DISCOVERING AMERICA

The Pacific

CALIFORNIA · HAWAII

By
Thomas G. Aylesworth
Virginia L. Aylesworth

CHELSEA HOUSE PUBLISHERS
New York · Philadelphia

3   5   7   9   8   6   4   2

Library of Congress Cataloging-in-Publication Data

Aylesworth, Thomas G.
   The Pacific: California, Hawaii
Thomas G. Aylesworth, Virginia L. Aylesworth.
      p. cm.—(Discovering America)
      Includes bibliographical references and index.
      Summary: Discusses the geographical, historical, and cultural aspects of
California and Hawaii.
      ISBN 0-7910-3407-0.
         0-7910-3425-9 (pbk.)
      1. Pacific States—Juvenile literature. 2. California—Juvenile literature. 3. Hawaii—Juvenile
literature. [1. Pacific States. 2. California. 3. Hawaii.] I. Aylesworth, Virginia L. II. Title. III.
Series: Aylesworth, Thomas G. Discovering America.

F851.A95   1995   94-45822
979.4—dc20   CIP
                                             AC

CONTENTS

HAWAII 61

California

The state seal of California was first adopted in 1849. Since then it has been redesigned, with the present seal adopted in 1937. Minerva, the Roman goddess of wisdom, war, arts, and handicrafts, is seated. The bear in front of Minerva's shield is a symbol of the early American settlers' struggle for independence and, as such, is a reminder of the bear flag revolt of 1846. Ships in the background represent commerce; a sheaf of wheat and clusters of grapes stand for agriculture. The Sierra Nevada mountains are pictured in the distance and a miner at work can be seen on the shore. The state motto appears beneath a semi-circle of 31 stars, representing the number of states in the Union after the admission of California. Printed around the outer circle are the words The Great Seal of the State of California.

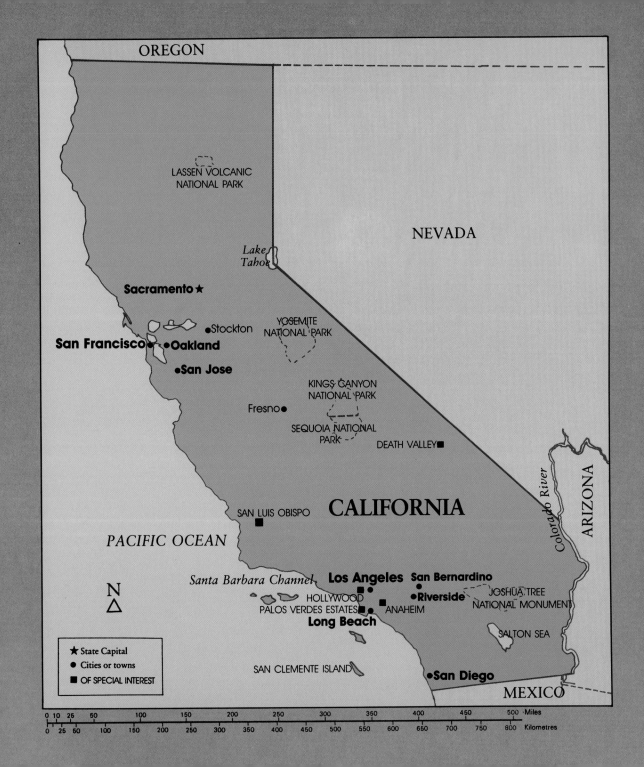

CALIFORNIA

At a Glance

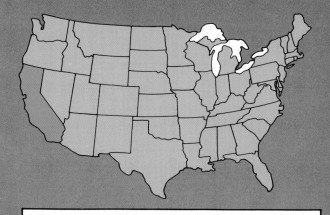

Capital: Sacramento

State Bird: California Valley Quail

State Motto: *Eureka* (I Have Found It)

State Tree: California Redwood

State Song: "I Love You, California"

Size: 158,706 square miles (3rd largest)
Population: 30,866,851 (nation's largest)

Nickname: Golden State

State Flag

State Flower: Golden Poppy

Major Crops: Grapes, cotton, flowers, citrus fruits, vegetables, melons, almonds, olives

Major Industries: Agriculture, manufacturing (transportation equipment, processed foods, electrical machinery), aerospace, petroleum

State Flag

The state flag of California was adopted in 1911. In the center of a white field is a brown grizzly bear on a patch of green grass. A horizontal red stripe runs along the bottom of the flag, with "California Republic" printed above it. A five-pointed star, representing sovereignty, appears in the upper left corner. The colors of the flag are symbolic; white standing for purity and red for courage.

State Motto
Eureka

The Greek motto, meaning "I have found it," refers to the state's admission to the Union and to the discovery of gold.

A view of the Santa Monica Beach in Southern California.

State Capital
Sacramento has been the state capital since 1854. Prior to that, Monterey, San Jose, Vallejo, Benecia, and San Francisco were used briefly as capitals.

State Name and Nickname
Spanish explorers named California after an imaginary island in a 16th-century novel, *The Deeds of Esplandián,* by Garci Ordoñez de Montalvo.

The official nickname of California, *The Golden State,* was chosen in 1968. It refers to the discovery of gold at Sutter's mill in 1848, to the fields of yellow poppies that bloom in the spring, and to California's brilliant sunshine.

State Fish
In 1947, the California golden trout, *Salmo aquabonita,* was named state fish.

State Tree
California redwood, *Sequoia sempervirens* and *Sequoia gigantea,* were designated state trees in 1937.

State Bird
The California valley quail, *Lophortyx californica,* was selected state bird by popular vote in 1931.

State Animal
The California grizzly bear, *Ursus californicus,* was chosen state animal in 1953.

State Flower
The state legislature designated the golden poppy, *Eschscholtzia californica,* state flower in 1903.

State Fossil
The California saber-toothed cat, *Smilodon californicus,* was named state fossil in 1973.

State Insect
In 1972, the California dog-face butterfly, *Zerene eurydice,* was chosen state insect.

State Marine Mammal
The California gray whale, *Eschrichtius robustus,* was designated state marine mammal in 1975.

State Mineral
Gold was selected state mineral in 1965.

State Reptile
In 1972, the California desert tortoise, *Gopherus agassizi,* was chosen state reptile.

State Rock
Serpentine was named state rock in 1965.

State Song
"I Love You, California," with words by F. B. Silverwood and music by A. F. Frankenstein, is the state song of California. Although it was first introduced in 1913, it was not officially adopted by the state legislature until 1951.

Population
The population of California in 1992 was 30,866,851, making it the most populous state in the nation. There are

181.79 people per square mile.

Industries

The principal industries of the state are agriculture, services, manufacturing, and trade. The chief manufactured products are foods, primary and fabricated metals, machinery, electric and electronic equipment, and transportation equipment.

Agriculture

The chief crops of the state are grapes, cotton, oranges, hay, tomatoes, lettuce, strawberries, almonds, broccoli, walnuts, sugar beets, peaches, and potatoes. California is also a livestock state, and there are estimated to be 8.17 million cattle and calves, 250,000 hogs and pigs, 945,000 sheep and lambs, and 27.6 million chickens on its farms. Fir, pine, redwood, and oak are harvested for timber. Asbestos, boron minerals, cement, diatomite, calcined, gypsum, construction sand and gravel are important mineral products. Commercial fishing earned $136.3 million in 1992.

Sports

California is a hotbed of sports activity. On the collegiate level, the NCAA baseball championship has been won by the University of California (1947, 1957), USC (1948, 1958, 1961, 1963, 1968, 1970-74, 1978), Cal State Fullerton (1979, 1984), and Stanford University (1987-88). In basketball, Stanford (1942), University of San Francisco (1955-56), California (1959), and UCLA (1964-65, 1967-73, 1975) have won the NCAA tournament, while San Francisco (1949), Fresno State University (1983), and UCLA (1985) have won the National Invitation Tournament. Football's Rose Bowl game is held in Pasadena every year. California, USC, Stanford, and UCLA have each won several times over the years. Santa Clara University has triumphed in the Orange Bowl (1950) and the Sugar

An elaborate sand castle dominates the landscape at this San Diego beach.

Bowl (1937-38), while St. Mary's was victorious in the Cotton Bowl in 1939.

On the professional level, California is represented by numerous teams in the four major sports. In baseball, the Los Angeles Dodgers play their home games in Dodger Stadium, the San Diego Padres in San Diego/Jack Murphy Stadium, the San Francisco Giants in Candlestick Park, the Oakland Athletics in the Oakland Coliseum, and the California Angels in Anaheim Stadium, which they share with the Los Angeles Rams of the National Football League. The NFL's Los Angeles Raiders play in the Memorial Coliseum, while the San Francisco 49ers play in Candlestick Park and the San Diego Chargers in San Diego/Jack Murphy Stadium. National Basketball Association teams based in California include the Los Angeles Lakers, who play in the Great Western Forum, the Los Angeles Clippers (Memorial Sports Arena), the Golden State Warriors (Oakland Coliseum Arena), and the Sacramento Kings (ARCO Arena). The Los Angeles Kings of the National Hockey League also perform in the Great Western Forum, while the San Jose Sharks play in the Cow Palace.

Government

The governor of California is elected to a four-year term, as are the lieutenant governor, secretary of state, attorney general, treasurer, controller, and superintendent of public instruction. The voters also elect a five-member State Board of Equalization. The state legislature, whose sessions begin in even-numbered years and last for two years, consists of a 40-member senate and an 80-member assembly. Senators serve four-year terms and are elected from senatorial districts; assembly members serve two-year terms and are elected from assembly districts. The most recent state constitution was adopted in 1879. In addition to its two U.S. senators, California has 52 representatives in the U.S. House of Representatives.

Major Cities

Los Angeles (population 3,485,398). In 1781, Don Felipe de Neve, Governor of California, founded El Pueblo de Nuestra Señora La Reina de Los Angeles de Porciuncula— "The Town of Our Lady the Queen of the Angels of Porciuncula." With the seizure of California by the United States in 1846, the town was transformed into a thriving frontier community. Its growth received a tremendous boost from the gold rush of 1849. The rise of the motion picture industry after 1910 was a major factor in the increase in population. The population doubled in the 1920s, setting the stage for even greater growth in the years to come, and by 1940 it had surpassed the 1.5 million mark.

Los Angeles has had severe racial confrontations in its recent history. In August 1965, rioting broke out in the predominantly black suburb of Watts. Rioters burned buildings, looted stores, and shot at firemen and police. The riots lasted for several days and resulted in 35 deaths, injury to several hundred others, and property damage. The National Guard was called in to restore order.

In 1992, riots erupted in South Central Los Angeles after a California jury acquitted four police officers on all but one count in the brutal beating of a black motorist, Rodney King. This videotaped attack was shown throughout the nation on television news broadcasts. The riots resulted in 52 deaths and damage estimated at over $1 billion. Army and Marine National Guard units were called in to restore order and to help residents seek federal funds and help rebuild businesses.

Los Angeles continues to grow today, and despite its natural disasters and racial strife, it has become a major scientific, artistic, and cultural community.

Places to visit in Los Angeles: City Hall, Music Center of Los Angeles County, Los Angeles Children's Museum, Museum of Contemporary Art, Wells Fargo History Museum, Little Tokyo, Chinatown, Los Angeles Temple Visitors Center, El Pueblo de Los Angeles Historic Park, Avila Adobe, Old Plaza Firehouse, Olvera Street, Sepulveda House (1887), Griffith Park, Los Angeles Zoo, UCLA Botanical Garden, Elysian Park, Descanso Gardens, Los Angeles State and County Arboretum, Exposition Park, Los Angeles Memorial Coliseum, Natural History Museum of Los Angeles County, California Museum of Science and Industry, Lummis Home and Garden State Historical Monument, Southwest Museum, South Coast Botanic Garden, Farmers Market, Will Rogers State Historic Park, Los Angeles County Museum of Art, George C. Page La Brea Discoveries Museum, Rancho La Brea Tar Pits, CBS Television City, Paramount Film and Television Studios, Simon Rodia Towers, Wight Art Gallery, and the Junior Arts Center.

Sacramento (population 369,365). Sacramento was settled in 1839 by Captain John Sutter on a 50,000-acre land grant from the Mexican government. The present-day

The Rose Bowl, one of the most important games in college football, is held annually at Pasadena, California.

Hollywood's Sunset Strip is one of the most famous streets in the country.

city was laid out on Sutter's property in 1848. When gold was found on the land that same year, the city rapidly grew into a major supply center. It was chosen state capital in 1854.

Transportation facilities were important in the growth of Sacramento. In 1860 the western terminus of the Pony Express was established in Sacramento, and in 1863 the Central Pacific Railroad began laying tracks from Sacramento over the Sierra Nevada to meet the Union Pacific Railroad. This led to the creation of the first transcontinental rail route in 1869. Today missile development and the nearby McClellan Air Force Base and Sacramento Army Depot boost the city's economy.

Places to visit in Sacramento: State Capitol, California Vietnam Veterans Memorial, Crocker Art Museum, Old Governor's Mansion, Old Sacramento Historic District, B. F. Hastings Museum, California State Railroad Museum, Central Pacific Railroad Station Museum, Old Eagle Theatre, Sacramento History Center, Sacramento Science Center, State Archives, State Library, Sutter's Fort State Historic Park, State Indian Museum, Towe Ford Museum, Waterworld USA, Fairytale Town, and the Sacramento Zoo.

San Diego (population 1,110,554). The Portuguese conquistador Juan Rodriguez Cabrillo landed in San Diego Bay on September 28, 1542, and called this site San Miguel. Don Sebastián Vizcaino renamed it San Diego in 1602, and in 1769 the first mission in California was built here by Gasper de Portolá. California's southernmost city has a Mexican flavor due to its proximity to the border town of Tijuana. Growth in the area was slow until after California achieved statehood in 1850. In recent years, San Diego has become a major metropolitan center, as well as a popular year-round resort city. In the mid-1970s it displaced San Francisco as California's second largest city. It is the home of the 11th Naval District, and it is a growing oceanography center. It is also noted for avocado producing, electronics, manufacturing, education, health and biomedical research, tourism, and ship, aircraft, and missile building.

Places to visit in San Diego: Mission Basilica San Diego de Alcalá, Presidio Park, Junípero Serra Museum, Whaley House (1856), Old Town San Diego State Historic Park, Gaslamp Quarter, Balboa Park, San Diego Zoo, Natural History Museum, Reuben H. Fleet Space Theater and Science Center, San Diego Aerospace Museum, International Aerospace Hall of Fame, San Diego Museum of Art, Timken Art Gallery, Museum of Photographic Arts, San Diego Hall of Champions, Museum of Man, Old Globe Theatre, Spanish Village Arts and Crafts Center, Seaport Village, Villa Montezuma/ Jesse Shepard House (1887), Sea World, Embarcadero, Mission Bay Park, and San Diego Wild Animal Park.

San Francisco (population 723,959). Founded in 1776 by Spanish explorer Juan Bautista de Anza, San Francisco is an "air-conditioned city," with warm winters and cool summers. The discovery of gold at Sutter's mill in 1848 had a tremendous impact on the growth of the city. It became an important port and supply depot for miners in their search for gold, with its population blossoming from 800 in 1848 to 25,000 the following year. Despite suffering millions of dollars in damage caused by a devastating earthquake in 1906, and experiencing numerous earthquakes and tremors since then, the city has continued to prosper. An earthquake in October 1989 took 62 lives and caused extensive damage, including the collapse of a 30-foot section of the San Francisco-Oakland Bay Bridge.

San Francisco is noted for the beauty of its setting. Surrounded on three sides by the Pacific Ocean, the San Francisco Bay, and the Golden Gate, it occupies the tip of a narrow and hilly peninsula and a number of its structures are built on the edge of hillsides.

Balboa Park in San Diego encompasses 1,400 acres and is the location for many of the city's museums, as well as the San Diego Zoo.

Today, San Francisco is an important financial, industrial, and cultural center and a melting pot of cultures from around the world.

Places to visit in San Francisco:
Twin Peaks, Mission Dolores (1776), City Hall, Performing Arts Center, War Memorial/Opera House, Cow Palace, Haas-Lilienthal House (1886), Japan Center, Golden Gate Bridge, Palace of Fine Arts, Acres of Orchids, Cable Car Museum, Society of California Pioneers Museum and Library, San Francisco Museum of Modern Art, Wells Fargo Bank History Museum, Treasure Island Museum, Randall Museum, National Maritime Museum, Exploratorium, California Palace of Legion of Honor, M. H. de Young Memorial Museum, Asian Art Museum, California Academy of Sciences, Natural History Museum and Aquarium, Mexican Museum, Old Mint, Alcatraz Island, Embarcadero, Chinatown, Telegraph Hill, Fisherman's Wharf, Presidio, Ghiradelli Square, Pier 39, and San Francisco Zoo.

Home to about thirty fishing vessels, Fisherman's Wharf in San Francisco is a popular visiting spot for seafood-loving tourists.

Places To Visit
The National Park Service maintains 18 areas in the state of California: Cabrillo National Monument, Death Valley National Monument, Devils Postpile National Monument, Joshua Tree National Monument, Lava Beds National Monument, Muir Woods National Monument, Pinnacles National Monument, Channel Islands National Park, Lassen Volcanic National Park, Sequoia and Kings Canyon National Parks, Yosemite National Park, Redwood National Park, Point Reyes National Seashore, Whiskeytown-Shasta-Trinity National Recreation Area, Golden Gate National Recreation Area, John Muir National Historical Site, and Fort Point National Historic Site. In addition, there are 86 state recreation areas.
Alturas: Modoc County Historical Museum. Exhibits include Indian artifacts and an extensive firearms collection.

Anaheim: Disneyland. This 80-acre park is divided into seven main sections: Main Street, USA; Fantasyland; Tomorrowland; Adventureland; Frontierland; New Orleans Square; and, Critter Country.

Arcadia: Los Angeles State and County Arboretum. This horticultural research center contains 127 acres of plants from around the world, as well as several historic buildings.

Auburn: Placer County Museum. Old mining equipment, weapons, and old photographs depict the early days of Placer County.

Bakersfield: Kern County Museum. Visitors may tour this 15-acre village containing many restored buildings, including a Queen Anne mansion, wooden jail, hotel, and saloon.

Barstow: Calico Ghost Town Regional Park. This restored 1880s mining town includes a general store, a schoolhouse, and the Maggie Mine.

Berkeley: Judah L. Magnes Museum. This museum houses artistic, historical, and literary materials tracing Jewish life throughout the world.

Bishop: Laws Railroad Museum and Historical Site.

The sheer face of Half-Dome Mountain in Yosemite National Park (established in 1890) attracts many mountain climbers.

Disneyland is a favorite vacation spot for people of all ages.

Visitors may tour a post office containing vintage equipment and a restored station-agent's house.

Bridgeport: Bodie State Historic Park. Fires in 1892 and 1932 destroyed all but a few buildings in this unrestored, late-1800s ghost town.

Buena Park: Knott's Berry Farm. An Old West Ghost Town, Fiesta Village, Wild Water Wilderness, and Camp Snoopy are featured in California's oldest amusement park.

Calistoga: Old Faithful Geyser of California. This geyser, fed by an underground river, erupts every 40 minutes, sending thousands of gallons of water 60 feet in the air.

Carmel: Mission San Carlos Borromeo del Río Carmelo. Founded in 1770 by Father Junípero Serra, this mission was the priest's home until his death in 1784.

Desert Hot Springs: Cabot's Old Indian Pueblo and Museum. This four-story Hopi Indian-style mansion features Indian and Eskimo artifacts.

Escondido: Lawrence Welk Theatre-Museum. This museum contains mementos from the career of the well-known bandleader.

Fairfield: Western Railway Museum. Visitors may take a two-mile ride on a streetcar, and tour a museum containing 100 antique trains and railroad cars.

Fort Bragg: California Western Railroad. A 40-mile round trip on a train affectionately known as the "Skunk" takes passengers through groves of redwood trees along the Noyo River.

Fremont: Mission San José. This adobe church, reconstructed after the original was destroyed by an earthquake, contains the original baptismal font, statues, and historic vestments.

Fresno: The Discovery Center. This family-oriented museum features hands-on science exhibits and American Indian artifacts.

Garden Grove: Crystal Cathedral. This church, designed by Philip Johnson, resembles a four-pointed crystal star.

Hollywood: Mann's Chinese Theatre. The handprints and footprints of many movie stars can be seen in the cement at the entrance to this theater.

La Jolla: Scripps Aquarium-Museum. This aquarium-museum features a marine life exhibit and an onshore tidepool.

Lompoc: Mission La Purísima Concepción State Historic Park. Indian artifacts and mission relics are displayed in this restored mission, originally founded in 1787.

Long Beach: *Queen Mary.* Visitors may tour the wheelhouse, officer's quarters, salons, and engine room of this historic ship.

Malibu: J. Paul Getty Museum. This recreation of an ancient Roman villa contains Greek and Roman antiquities, and pre-20th-century paintings, drawings, and sculptures.

Marina Del Rey: Fisherman's

Village. This is a model of a turn-of-the-century New England fishing village.

Modesto: McHenry Museum. Historical exhibits are displayed in period rooms, including a schoolroom, blacksmith shop, and doctor's office.

Monterey: Monterey State Historic Park. The buildings in this park include the

Many Hollywood actors and actresses hope to have their handprints, footprints, and signatures displayed at the forecourt of Mann's Chinese Theatre, as a symbol of their stardom status.

Robert Louis Stevenson House and California's First Theater.

Morgan Hill: Wagons to Wings Museum. This museum houses wagons, coaches, and planes of various types, including many one-of-a-kind vehicles.

Oakland: Oakland Museum. This complex of galleries and gardens features exhibits on the natural science, history, and art of California.

Oceanside: Camp Pendleton. This 125,000-acre Marine Corps base serves as an ecological preserve, in addition to being one of the world's leading amphibious training camps.

The **Queen Mary,** *at one time one of the world's greatest transatlantic cruise ships, is now permanently docked in Long Beach.*

Miniature horses were first introduced in the 16th century, as pets for the royal courts in Europe. The Winners' Circle Ranch is the largest miniature horse ranch in the western U.S.; they breed the horses for competition in horse shows, and for sale.

Oroville: Chinese Temple. This temple, built in 1863, contains several chapels, a courtyard garden, and an assortment of collections.

Pacific Grove: John Steinbeck Memorial Museum. Originally belonging to Steinbeck's grandparents, this house contains memorabilia from the author's youth.

Palm Desert: The Living Desert. The beauty of the world's desert lands is preserved in this 1,200-acre wildlife and botanical park.

Palm Springs: Palm Springs Aerial Tramway. The world's longest double-reversible single span aerial tramway offers spectacular views of the San Jacinto Mountains.

Palo Alto: The Barbie Hall of Fame. This collection contains more than 10,000 Barbie dolls and accessories.

Palomar Mountain: Palomar Observatory. This is the home of the 200-inch Hale telescope, the largest in the United States.

Pasadena: Norton Simon Museum of Art. Works by Monet, Renoir, van Gogh, and Degas are displayed, together with southeast Asian and Indian sculpture.

Petaluma: Winners Circle Ranch. This ranch specializes in the breeding and training of miniature show horses.

Redding: Lake Shasta Caverns. A guided tour includes a boat ride across the McCloud Arm of Lake Shasta.

Riverside: California Museum of Photography. Among the displays are hands-on exhibits which demonstrate how motion pictures are made.

St. Helena: Silverado Museum. This museum contains memorabilia of author Robert Louis Stevenson, including photographs, letters, and original manuscripts.

San Jose: Winchester Mystery House. This 160-room mansion features stairways that go nowhere, trapdoors, and secret passageways.

San Juan Capistrano: Mission San Juan Capistrano. Known for its swallows, which leave each year on October 23rd and return on March 19th, this complex includes the Serra Chapel, which is the oldest building in California.

Sarah L. Winchester began building the Winchester Mystery House in 1884. Having been told by a psychic that she would not die as long as construction on the house continued, Sarah kept adding on to the house haphazardly until her death in 1922.

San Luis Obispo: Mission San Luis Obispo de Tolosa. Built in 1772, this mission still serves as a parish church.

San Marino: Huntington Library, Art Collection and Botanical Gardens. A copy of the Gutenberg Bible is among the rare books contained in this library.

San Mateo: Coyote Point Museum. This modern museum contains hands-on exhibits, dioramas, and a working beehive.

San Pedro: Ports O' Call Village. This recreation of a New England-style village contains 90 shops and restaurants.

San Simeon: Hearst San Simeon

State Historical Monument. The centerpiece of the 137-acre estate of publisher William Randolph Hearst is the magnificent Hearst Castle, surrounded by formal Renaissance gardens.

Santa Barbara: Mission Santa Barbara. Completed in 1820, this example of Spanish Renaissance architecture is one of the best preserved of the missions.

Santa Clara: Great America. This 100-acre theme park

The Mission Santa Barbara was founded in 1786 by Fermin Lasuen, a Franciscan priest. Twice restored after earthquake damage, the mission has not changed its appearance since 1820, and is generally considered the most beautiful in the chain of 21 missions in California.

Visitors on the public tours at Universal Studios get an inside look at the film industry, as well as a closeup view of this movie legend.

consists of five major areas: Hometown Square, Yukon Territory, Yankee Harbor, County Fair, and Orleans Place.

Santa Cruz: The Mystery Spot. The laws of gravity and perspective do not appear to apply in this 150-foot section of redwood forest.

Santa Monica: Angels Attic. This restored Victorian house is devoted to antique dolls, miniatures, and toys.

Santa Rosa: Luther Burbank Home and Gardens. Included in this home of the famed horticulturist is a greenhouse designed by Burbank himself.

Sausalito: Village Fair. Visitors may purchase locally-made handicrafts in specialty shops housed in this three-story building.

Solvang: Old Mission Santa Inés. Founded in 1804, this gold adobe building now contains a museum featuring religious artifacts.

Sonoma: Sonoma State Historic Park. This complex includes the Mission San Francisco Solano and the home of General Mariano Vallejo, founder of Sonoma.

Stockton: Pixie Woods Wonderland. This children's park offers theater programs, as well as rides and an animal petting zoo.

Truckee: Donner Memorial State Park. This 353-acre park is a memorial to the 89-person Donner party, which was stranded in the area by blizzards in the winter of 1846-47.

Universal City: Universal Studios Hollywood. Visitors may tour movie and television sets, and experience live action shows and special effects in California's largest and busiest studio.

Valencia: Six Flags Magic Mountain. This amusement park includes Tidal Wave, Ninja, Freefall, and Viper among its rides.

Vallejo: Marine World Africa USA. This oceanarium and

An orca, also called the killer whale, performs at Marine World.

African animal park features more than 1,000 animals in shows and natural settings.
Ventura: San Buenaventura Mission. This was the last mission founded by Father Junípero Serra.
Victorville: Roy Rogers-Dale Evans Museum. This museum contains memorabilia associated with the western film and television stars.

Events

There are many events and organizations that schedule seasonal activities of various kinds in the state of California. Here are some of them.

Sports: Horse racing at Santa Anita Park (Arcadia), MONY Tournament of Champions (Carlsbad), Bidwell Classic Marathon (Chico), Clovis Rodeo (Clovis), World Championship Crab Races and Crab Feed (Crescent City), Gasquet Raft Race (Crescent City), Jumping Frog Jamboree (Del Mar), horse racing at the County Fairgrounds (Del Mar), Blue Angels Golf Tournament (El Centro), Cross-Country Kinetic Sculpture Race (Eureka), White Water Races (Kernville), Kernville Rod Run (Kernville), Great Livermore Airshow (Livermore), Vandenberg AFB Missile Competition and Open House (Lompoc), Toyota Grand Prix (Long Beach), Boat Parades (Long Beach), USA/Mobil Outdoor Track and Field Championships (Los Angeles), Stampede Days (Marysville), West Coast Antique Fly-in (Merced), AT&T Pebble Beach National Pro-Am Golf Championship (Monterey), auto and motorcycle racing at Laguna Seca Raceway (Monterey), skiing at Mt. Shasta Ski Park (Mt. Shasta), Father's Day Bicycle Tour (Nevada City), PRCA Rodeo (Oakdale), Quarter Horse Show (Oakdale), California Dally Team Roping Championships (Oakdale), Tennis Tournament (Ojai), Oxnard Airshow (Oxnard), Bob Hope Chrysler Classic (Palm Desert), Mounted Police Rodeo and Parade (Palm Springs), sled dog races (Palm Springs), Nabisco Dinah Shore Invitational (Palm Springs), World Wrist Wrestling Championships (Petaluma), Red Bluff Roundup (Red Bluff), Red Bluff Boat Drags (Red Bluff), Exchange Club Air Show (Redding), Rodeo Week (Redding), Water Festival (Sacramento), California Rodeo (Salinas), International Airshow (Salinas), Grand National Rodeo, Horse Show and Livestock Exposition (San Francisco), Firefighters Rodeo (San Jose), San Benito County Saddle Horse Show Parade and Rodeo (San Juan Bautista), horse racing at Bay Meadows Racecourse (San Mateo), Summer Sports Festival (Santa Barbara), National Horse and Flower Show (Santa Barbara), Parade of Champions (Santa Clara), Elks Rodeo and Parade (Santa Maria), Sports and Arts Festival (Santa Monica), sled dog races (Truckee), cross-country skiing marathon (Truckee), Truckee-Tahoe Airshow (Truckee), Rodeo (Truckee), Whaleboat Regatta (Vallejo), Whale Watching (Ventura).

Arts and Crafts: Colony Days (Atascadero), Art Festival (Catalina Island), Whole Earth Festival (Davis), Winter Festival (Laguna Beach), Sawdust Festival (Laguna Beach), Fall Festival (Livermore), Cinco de Mayo Celebration (Los Angeles), Old Adobe Fiesta (Petaluma), Children's Lawn Festival (Redding), The Great American Arts Festival (San Jose), Renaissance Faire (San Luis Obispo), Rainbow of Gems and Earth Science Show (Santa Maria), Villa Montalvo Lively Arts Festival (Saratoga), Sausalito Art Festival (Sausalito).

Music: Calico Spring Festival (Barstow), Carmel Bach Festival (Carmel), Russian River Jazz

Festival (Guerneville),
Symphony Under the Stars
(Hollywood), Long Beach Blues
Festival (Long Beach), Long
Beach Symphony (Long Beach),
Grand Opera (Long Beach), Civic
Light Opera and Ballet (Long
Beach), Los Angeles Music
Center Opera (Los Angeles),
Mendocino Festival of Music
(Mendocino), Central California
Band Review (Merced),
Monterey Jazz Festival
(Monterey), Ojai Music Festival
(Ojai), Oakland Ballet (Oakland),
Old Time Fiddlers' Contest
(Oroville), Marching Band
Festival (Pacific Grove), Shasta
Dixieland Jazz Festival
(Redding), Dixieland Jazz
Festival (Sacramento), Music
Circus (Sacramento), Spreckels
Outdoor Organ (San Diego), San
Francisco Ballet (San Francisco),
Midsummer Music Festival (San
Francisco), San Francisco Opera
(San Francisco), San Francisco
Symphony Orchestra (San
Francisco), San Jose Symphony
(San Jose), Mozart Festival (San
Luis Obispo), Cabrillo Music
Festival (Santa Cruz), Music at
the Vineyards (Saratoga), Jazz on
the Waterfront (Stockton).

Entertainment: Fandango
Celebration (Alturas), Modoc
Last Frontier Fair (Alturas),
Contra Costa County Fair
(Antioch), Wild West Stampede
(Auburn), Gold Panning Show

This happy cook prepares her fare for the Gilroy Garlic Festival.

(Auburn), Placer County Fair (Auburn), Gold Country Fair (Auburn), Museum Heritage Days (Bakersfield), Kern County Fair (Bakersfield), Calico Hullabaloo (Barstow), Calico Spring Festival (Barstow), Calico Days (Barstow), Cherry Festival (Beaumont), Tri-County Fair (Bishop), Colorado River County Fairs (Blythe), Liar's Contest (Borrego Springs), Borrego Days Festival (Borrego Springs), Silverado Days Celebration (Buena Park), Napa County Fair (Calistoga), Pioneer Days (Chico), Silver Dollar Fair (Chico), Expo Fair (Chico), Highland Gathering and Games (Costa Mesa), Orange County Fair (Costa Mesa), Easter in July Lily Festival (Crescent City), Jamboree Days (Crestline), Picnic Day (Davis), Del Mar Fair (Del Mar), Railroad Days (Dunsmuir), Brawley Cattle Call (El Centro), Rhododendron Festival (Eureka), Whale Festival (Fort Bragg), Rhododendron Show (Fort Bragg), Salmon Barbecue (Fort Bragg), Paul Bunyan Days (Fort Bragg), Swedish Festival (Fresno), Obon-Odori Festival (Fresno), Christmas Tree Lane (Fresno), Gilroy Garlic Festival (Gilroy), Nevada County Fair (Grass Valley), Cornish Christmas (Grass Valley), Farmers Fair (Hemet),

Hollywood Christmas Parade (Hollywood), National Date Festival (Indio), Whiskey Flat Days (Kernville), Kernville Stampede (Kernville), Mission San Antonio de Padua Fiesta (King City), Great Sierra Winter Carnival (Lake Tahoe), Wagon Train Caravan (Lake Tahoe), Jeepers Jamboree (Lake Tahoe), Antelope Valley Fair and Alfalfa Festival (Lancaster), Alameda County Fair (Livermore), International Spring Festival (Lodi), Flower Festival (Lompoc), Founding Celebration (Lompoc), Chinese New Year

(Los Angeles), Hanamatsuri (Los Angeles), Asian Cultural Festival (Los Angeles), Nisei Week (Los Angeles), Los Angeles County Fair (Los Angeles), Bok Kai Festival (Marysville), California Prune Festival (Marysville), Mendocino Coast Food and Winefest (Mendocino), Merced County Fair (Merced), Ripon Almond Blossom Festival (Modesto), Graffiti Night (Modesto), Monterey County Fair (Monterey), Spring Fair (Napa), Town and Country Fair (Napa), Constitution Day Parade (Nevada City), Fall Color

A parade of flowers sweeps through the streets of Pasadena to celebrate the annual Rose Bowl.

Spectacular (Nevada City), Victorian Christmas (Nevada City), Newport Seafest (Newport Beach), Christmas Boat Parade (Newport Beach), Strawberry Festival (Oxnard), Channel Islands Harbor Parade of Lights (Oxnard), Good Ole Days and Victorian Home Tour (Pacific Grove), Wildflower Show (Pacific Grove), Feast of Lanterns (Pacific Grove), Butterfly Parade (Pacific Grove), Tournament of Roses (Pasadena), California Mid-State Fair (Paso Robles), Mission San Miguel Arcángel Fiesta (Paso Robles), Sonoma-Marin Fair (Petaluma), Wagon Train Week (Placerville), El Dorado County Fair (Placerville), Los Angeles County Fair (Pomona), Plumas County Fair (Quincy), Grape Harvest Festival (Rancho Cucamonga), Tehama County Fair (Red Bluff), Shasta District Fair (Redding), San Mateo County Fair and Floral Fiesta (Redwood City), Camellia Festival (Sacramento), California State Fair (Sacramento), National Orange Show (San Bernardino), San Clemente Summer Fiesta (San Clemente), Corpus Christi Fiesta (San Diego), Festival of Bells (San Diego), Admission Day (San Diego), Cabrillo Festival (San Diego), Christmas on the Prado (San Diego), Christmas-Light Boat Parade (San Diego), Blossom Festival (San Diego), Chinese New Year (San Francisco), Cherry Blossom Festival (San Francisco), San Francisco Fair and Exposition (San Francisco), Santa Clara County Fair (San Jose), Early Days Celebration (San Juan Bautista), Festival of Whales (San Juan Capistrano), Fiesta de las Golondrinas (San Juan Capistrano), Adiós a las Golondrinas (San Juan Capistrano), Poly Royal (San Luis Obispo), La Fiesta de San Luis Obispo (San Luis Obispo), Renaissance Faire (San Luis Obispo), San Mateo County Fair and Floral Fiesta (San Mateo), Santa Barbara International Orchid Show (Santa Barbara), Old Spanish Days Fiesta (Santa Barbara), Civil War Reenactment (Santa Cruz), National Begonia Festival (Santa Cruz), Santa Cruz County Fair (Santa Cruz), Santa Barbara County Fair (Santa Maria), Luther Burbank Rose Festival (Santa Rosa), Sonoma County Fair (Santa Rosa), Scottish Gathering and Games (Santa Rosa), Danish Days Festival (Solvang), Valley of the Moon Vintage Festival (Sonoma), Fireman's Muster (Sonora), Mother Lode Round-Up (Sonora), Mother Lode Fair (Sonora), Stockton Asparagus Festival (Stockton), San Joaquin County Fair (Stockton), Obon Festival and Bazaar (Stockton), Greek Festival (Stockton), Lassen County Fair (Susanville), Conejo Valley Days (Thousand Oaks), Stanislaus County Fair (Turlock), Mendocino County Fair and Apple Show (Ukiah), Solano County Fair (Vallejo), Ventura County Fair (Ventura), Huck Finn Jubilee (Victorville), San Bernardino County Fair (Victorville).

Tours: Mine tours (Antioch), Catalina tours (Avalon), Eureka's Image Tours (Eureka), Jughandle Ecological Staircase (Fort Bragg), NBC Studios (Burbank), Adobe Tour (Monterey), Victorian Home Tour (Pacific Grove), Gold Bug Mine (Placerville), Naval Ship Tour (San Diego), San Francisco Bay Cruises (San Francisco), Tour of Old Adobes (San Juan Capistrano), gold prospecting tours (Sonora), agricultural tours (Visalia).

Theater: The Greek Theatre (Berkeley), Lawrence Welk Theater-Museum (Escondido), Ramona Pageant (Hemet), Laguna Moulton Playhouse (Laguna Beach), Greek Theatre in Griffith Park (Los Angeles), Foothill Theatre Company (Nevada City), Woodminster Summer Amphitheater (Oakland), Paramount Theatre (Oakland), Old Globe Theatre (San Diego), Performing Arts Center (San Francisco).

Northwestern California has a mountainous landscape of steep, tree-covered hills broken by gorges and valleys.

The Land and the Climate

California is perhaps the most diverse state in scenery, character, and climate. It is divided into eight main land regions: the Klamath Mountains, the Coast Ranges, the Central Valley, the Cascade Mountains, the Sierra Nevada, the Basin and Range Region, the Los Angeles Ranges, and the San Diego Ranges.

The Klamath Mountains are located in the northwestern corner of the state, a region that contains several small, tree-covered ranges that are steeper than the coastal mountains to the south. Deep canyons separate the peaks here, some of which rise from 6,000 to 8,000 feet above sea level. The area has a few valleys that are flat enough to be farmed, but its most important industry is forest products.

The Coast Ranges extend along the Pacific Coast from the Klamath Mountains to the Santa Barbara area. They include the Diablo, Santa Cruz, and Santa Lucia Ranges. The valleys in this region support livestock ranches, orchards, vineyards, and truck farms. Prominent among these valleys are the Napa Valley north of San Francisco, and the Santa Clara and Salinas Valleys south of the city. The famous California redwood tree grows only in the northern Coast Ranges.

Running through the earth of the Coast Ranges is the nation's largest fault, or break in the continuity of underlying rock formations. Movements of the earth's crust along such faults cause earthquakes. California's San Andreas Fault stretches from the Pacific Ocean near Point Arena southeastward into Southern California. It makes this area vulnerable to earthquakes, one of which almost destroyed San Francisco in 1906.

Above:
The climate and soil of northern California resemble those of the famous wine-making provinces of France. The similarity of the grapes grown, as well as the techniques used for blending, aging, and storage, make many California wines much like those of France.

At left:
The fertile soil of the Napa and Sonoma Valleys, north of San Francisco, is ideal for growing a wide range of fruits and vegetables. The area is perhaps best known for producing some of California's finest wine—a leading industry in many parts of the state.

California's famous redwoods are the earth's oldest and tallest trees. They grow along the northwest coast in a region that is affected by sea fog and cool summer breezes. Forests cover more than 40 percent of the state and are one of California's greatest natural resources.

The Central Valley, often called the Great Valley, is located east of the Coast Ranges. The valley has two major river systems—in the north, the Sacramento River system and in the south, the San Joaquin. The length of the valley is about 500 miles, and it extends from northwest to southeast, resembling a broad, open plain. Most of it is quite level, and it is the most fertile farming area west of the Rocky Mountains. The valley contains 60 percent of California's farmland, and almost every kind of crop can be raised here, including fruit, walnuts, asparagus, and hay. Central Valley ranchers raise beef and dairy cattle, sheep, poultry, and other livestock.

At left:
Boaters enjoy an outing on Lake Shasta, one of California's largest man-made lakes. Mount Shasta, seen in the distance, rises to a height of 14,162 feet and is covered with snow throughout the year.

Below:
Sequoia National Park, in the Sierra Nevada, is home to the giant redwoods known as *sequoia gigantea*. These trees are famous for the great size of their trunks (as much as 38 feet in diameter), although they are not as tall as the Coast, or California, redwood.

The Cascade Mountains stretch northward from the Central Valley and are located east of the Klamath Mountains. These mountains are the only ones in the state that were formed by volcanoes, one of which, Lassen Peak, 10,466 high, is still active. Mount Shasta, 14,162 feet high, was once an active volcano.

The Sierra Nevada (from the Spanish for "snow-covered mountain range") is east of the Central Valley, and stands like a rock wall more than 400 miles long and from 40 to 70 miles wide. Several of the mountains in the Sierra are more than 14,000 feet high, including Mount Whitney, at 14,495 feet—the highest point in the United States outside Alaska. In this region are deep canyons that were cut by rushing mountain rivers, especially in the western part of the Sierra. The most famous of these valleys is the Yosemite Valley, which was cut first by rivers and then by glaciers that formed the sheer granite cliffs that are such a tourist attraction.

Death Valley, on California's border with Nevada, is arid and forbidding. An average annual rainfall of only 3 inches renders it barren and unsuitable for any type of agriculture. The highest temperature ever recorded in North America, 134 degrees Fahrenheit, was registered in Death Valley.

The Basin and Range Region occupies much of southeastern California and part of the northeast as well, extending into Nevada, Oregon, and several other states. Most of the northern section is a huge lava plateau created when lava poured from great cracks in the earth thousands of years ago, flooding the area. The southern section of the region is still largely wilderness, including the beautiful Mojave and Colorado Deserts. Irrigation has made several valleys in southeastern California suitable for farming, notably the Imperial and Coachella Valleys, near the Mexican border. The most desolate part of the Basin and Range Region is Death Valley, near the California-Nevada border. Part of the valley is 282 feet below sea level, making it the lowest point in North America.

The Los Angeles Ranges are a small group of mountain ranges extending between Santa Barbara and San Diego Counties. They are sometimes called the Transverse Ranges, because they extend in an east-west direction. Among these ranges are the Santa Ynez, Santa

Monica, San Gabriel, and San Bernardino Mountains. Some geographers also include the San Jacinto and Santa Ana Mountains in this group.

The San Diego Ranges are also called the Peninsular Ranges; they cover most of San Diego County in the southwestern corner of California. These ranges include the Agua, Tibia, Laguna, and Vallecito Mountains. The San Diego Ranges extend south into the Baja California peninsula of Mexico.

The Pacific coastline of California is 840 miles long if measured in a straight line, but when the shorelines of the many bays and inlets are included, the seashore is 3,427 miles long. California has two magnificent natural harbors—San Francisco and San Diego Bays—and also the smaller harbors of Humboldt and Monterey Bays. But the Coast Ranges rise from the shore in steep cliffs and terraces along much of the coast. Offshore are two major groups of islands. The small and rocky Farallon Islands are about 30 miles west of San Francisco. There are eight Channel Islands off the southern California coast, of which the best known is Catalina Island, a popular vacation spot.

San Diego's climate is regarded as one of the most comfortable and stable in the country. San Diego Bay is an excellent natural harbor that shelters thousands of recreational, commercial, and naval vessels each year.

The two longest rivers in the state are the Sacramento and the San Joaquin. The Sacramento flows from a point near Mount Shasta south through the Central Valley. The San Joaquin rises in the Sierra Nevada and flows northwest through the Central Valley. These two rivers meet northeast of San Francisco and flow west to San Francisco Bay. Some smaller rivers, like the Feather and the Mokelumne, flow from the eastern mountains into the Sacramento or the San Joaquin. The Colorado River forms the border between Southern California and Arizona. This river is used not only for irrigation of the desert, but also as a water supply for many southern California cities and towns.

The Golden Gate Bridge has become one of California's best-known symbols. It spans San Francisco Bay, the state's best natural harbor and the West Coast's most important port.

Southern California is renowned for its warm waters and powerful surf. Some 840 miles of Pacific coastline have done much to popularize surfing, which has become a major attraction for California's youth.

Yosemite National Park contains several spectacular waterfalls, including Ribbon Falls (1,612 feet), which is the highest in North America. Other high waterfalls in the park are Bridalveil, Illilouette, Nevada, Silver Strand, Vernal, and Upper and Lower Yosemite.

There are about 8,000 lakes in California. The deepest is Lake Tahoe, on the California-Nevada border, which has an average depth of 1,500 feet. Most of the desert lakes contain dissolved minerals, including potash and salt, that make the water undrinkable.

California has several markedly different climates, and almost any climatic condition can be found within a short drive from any part of the state. Thus, rainfall on the north coast can be as much as 100 inches a year, while the southwestern deserts have received as little as two inches, which is about as dry as land can get. Areas in the Sierra Nevada get as much as 500 inches of snowfall in a year. The snow is the source of complex irrigation and water-supply systems. It also provides some of the world's finest skiing grounds, including Squaw Valley, the scene of the 1960 Winter Olympics.

Lake Tahoe is California's deepest lake. The Tahoe area, located on the California-Nevada border, provides some of the best skiing in the country and is one of the nation's most popular vacation spots.

Los Angeles, with a population of more than 3 million, is the largest city in California. It is one of the state's most important business and commercial centers and an attraction for visitors who wish to explore the movie and television capital of the United States.

Death Valley, California, claims to have had the highest temperature recorded on the North American continent (134 degrees Fahrenheit). San Diego boasts one of the country's most stable climates, with an average for January of 55 degrees F. and an August average of 69 degrees F. The Los Angeles area has a dry, Mediterranean type of climate, with only about 16 inches of annual rainfall and almost perpetual sunshine. But periodic industrial smog is a problem. San Francisco has cool summers and mild winters; the temperature seldom gets above 70 degrees F. or below 50 degrees F. San Francisco's fogs, erratic and occasional, may blanket one part of the city while nearby areas have clear, sparkling skies. Still, the city has almost twice as many days of sun as of fog.

In northern California, the average for the warmest month is only about 60 degrees F. On the high mountain slopes it is never warm: it may even snow in June or July. As a result, the mountain valleys draw huge crowds from the lower valleys, where inland summer temperatures may average over 80 degrees F.

Mono Lake is one of California's largest salt-water lakes. Its strange natural sculptures, created by a combination of rock and salt, are unique in the state.

The History

Before the European explorers arrived, several tribes of Indians lived in what was to become California. They were dispersed mainly in the fertile parts of the region and were separated from each other by the deserts and high mountains, which also separated them from other tribes farther east. In the far northwestern region were the Hupa Indians. The Maidu occupied the central section, and the Yuma lived in the south. The Pomo were in what are now Lake, Mendocino, and Sonoma Counties. Other tribes in the territory included the Míwok, the Modoc, and the Mojave.

A basket crafted by the Chumash Indians, early natives of the Santa Barbara coastal region. The Chumash had a culturally advanced society and produced sophisticated tools and weapons, including harpoons and sea-going canoes.

Probably the first white man to see the coast of what is now California was Juan Rodríguez Cabrillo, a Portuguese explorer in the service of Spain. He had sailed north from New Spain (now Mexico) in 1542 to explore the Pacific coast, looking for rich cities and a passage from the Pacific Ocean to the Atlantic. Along the way he discovered San Diego Bay, where he anchored for a time before sailing farther north. Although Cabrillo died in 1543, his men continued the voyage, and they may have sailed as far north as present-day Oregon.

In 1579, during his historic voyage around the world, Sir Francis Drake, the English sea captain, followed the Pacific coast. He landed near San Francisco Bay and claimed the land for England, naming it New Albion. This disturbed the Spanish, who feared that they might lose the area to England, so they sent several exploring parties along the coast. One of these parties was led by Sebastián Vizcaíno in 1602; he named many landmarks along the coast and sent a glowing report to Philip III of Spain, urging colonization of the territory.

The Spaniards, following their usual colonial policy, began to establish missions and other settlements in Baja California, the peninsula south of present-day California that is now part of Mexico. In 1769 Captain Gaspar de Portolá, the governor of Baja California, led an expedition that established the first presidio, or military fort, at San Diego. The following year he established another at Monterey. Spanish settlers arrived at what was then called Yerba Buena (now San Francisco) in 1776, establishing a presidio and a mission. Later, other groups settled along the coast in pueblos, or villages.

The Russians had strong fur-trading interests in Alaska, and they decided to sail down the Pacific coast in quest of more furs, especially those of the sea otter, which abounded in California waters. They established Fort Ross on the northern California coast in 1812. Russian immigrants began to settle on the north coast and to set up additional forts and fur-trading posts. In 1823 the United States proclaimed the Monroe Doctrine, which declared that North and South America should be considered closed to European colonization, and in 1824 Russia agreed to limit its settlements in Alaska. But the Russians did not leave the California region until the early 1840s.

Fort Ross was the site of an early Russian settlement in California. Journeying south from their colony in Alaska in 1812, the Russians established this base on the northern California coast to expand their fur trade and to provide additional foodstuffs for the Alaska colony. After many unsuccessful attempts to make the settlement profitable, the fort was abandoned in 1841.

Meanwhile, Franciscan friars of the Roman Catholic Church were contributing to the Spanish settlement of southern California. Father Junípero Serra had established the first California mission for the Indians when he was with Portolá on his expedition of 1769. The mission was called San Diego de Alcalá; it was built near present-day San Diego. By 1823 the Franciscans had established a chain of 21 missions, each about a day's walk from the next. These missions were the beginnings not only of San Diego, but also of such cities as Los Angeles, Santa Barbara, and San Francisco. They also account for the fact that almost every natural feature in southern California has a Spanish name. The Spanish colonists traveled up and down the region from one mission to another on a road called El Camino Real (the Royal Highway), which still exists as U.S. Highway 101. Not only did the priests convert some Indians to Christianity, they also taught them farming, weaving, and other skills.

After Mexico won its independence from Spain in 1821, California became a province of Mexico (1822). The Spanish missions were not popular with many Californians, and in the early 1830s the Mexican Government started selling off the mission lands. By 1846 private citizens owned almost all the property. Beginning in 1825, Mexico had begun sending governors to California, which caused many Californians to rebel because their affairs were being run by outsiders. A group led by Pío Pico clashed with Mexican Government troops in 1831 during a revolt against the harsh rule of Governor Manuel Victoria. He was forced to resign and went back to Mexico, which weakened his government's hold on the region.

California had emerged as a sea trading center after the *Otter,* the first American sailing vessel to reach the coast from the East, appeared in California waters in 1796. The first American explorer to arrive in California by land was Jedediah Strong Smith, a trapper who crossed the deserts in the southeast in 1826. Others followed, including frontiersmen Christopher "Kit" Carson, Joseph Reddeford Walker, and Ewing Young.

San Diego de Alcalá is the oldest mission in California. Founded by the Franciscan explorer Junípero Serra in 1769, it was established to help the Spanish convert California Indians to Christianity. Many such mission settlements grew into some of the state's most prominent cities, including San Diego, Santa Barbara, and San Francisco.

In 1841 a sizable group of American settlers arrived in California by land—the first of many organized parties to come by wagon train. Of course, the Americans wanted California to join the United States, but the Mexican Government refused to sell the territory. Between 1844 and 1846, John C. Frémont, a United States Army officer and explorer, led two surveying parties of soldiers into California. In March 1846 the Mexicans, suspicious of his activities, ordered him to leave. Frémont's men were encamped near Monterey, and Frémont defied the Mexican order by raising the Stars and Stripes on Hawk's Peak, some 25 miles away. The Americans began to build a small fort there, and on May 13, 1846, the United States and Mexico went to war.

In June a group of American settlers who were unaware of the declaration of war captured the Mexican headquarters at Sonoma, in northern California. There they raised a home-made flag emblazoned with a star, a grizzly bear, and the words *California Republic,* in an action that became known as the Bear Flag Revolt. Frémont, Commodore Robert F. Stockton, and General Stephen Watts Kearny were the military leaders instrumental in winning the Mexican War of 1846–48. Mexico surrendered its claim to California in the Treaty of Guadalupe Hidalgo, and California became part of the United States (1848).

Just before the end of the war, James W. Marshall found gold in the American River at Sutter's Mill. The property belonged to John A. Sutter, a German pioneer trader who had received a large land grant in the Sacramento Valley. News of the discovery, made on January 24, 1848, spread quickly, and thousands of people arrived by land and sea to stake out their claims in the area. (The unfortunate Sutter lost the use of his property and became a bankrupt, one of the first victims of "gold fever.") But the "forty-niners" swelled the population of California from about 26,000 to 379,994 between 1848 and 1860, and many communities became boom towns. San Francisco in particular grew into a prosperous trade center almost overnight by supplying

John Charles Frémont, a Civil War general and the first Republican candidate for the presidency, is perhaps best known as the explorer who defied Mexico in an effort to claim California for the United States. He surveyed and mapped many parts of the state, ignoring repeated orders from Mexico to leave the region. Frémont's actions did much to precipitate the Mexican War of 1846–48. His record in the Mexican War was marred by a court-martial, and he lost the presidential election of 1856. His subsequent service in the Civil War was so severely criticized that he resigned from the army in 1864 and pursued various businesses, none of which gained him any financial success.

the influx of gold-seekers with food and equipment. The miners who scrambled into the Sierra foothills built a chain of settlements with odd and delightful names like Rough and Ready, Angels Camp, Chinese Camp, Fiddletown, Poker Flat, and Poverty Hill. In their heyday some of these settlements had as many as 40,000 people.

On September 9, 1850, California became the 31st state of the Union. After the Civil War ended in 1865, still more immigrants from the East began to arrive, looking for high wages and cheap land. In 1869 the first transcontinental railroad connected Sacramento with the East; a year later, California's population had risen to about 560,000.

Eliza Tibbets, who imported oranges from Brazil, started the boom
that filled southwestern California with citrus groves. It brought
hundreds of thousands of new settlers, especially from the Middle
West. In 1862 a Hungarian, Count Haraszthy, brought 100,000 cut-
tings of European grapevines to California and imported skilled vine-
yard and winery workers from France, Italy, and Germany to set out
the vines and make wine.

California grew rapidly during the early 1900s. Farming increased
with the introduction of irrigation. By 1910 Hollywood had become
the movie capital of the world, because the climate was conducive to

A view of San Francisco in
1849, the year in which "gold
fever" began to reach epi-
demic proportions. Within
months after gold was discovered at Sutter's Mill, tens of
thousands of fortune-seekers
poured into California from
all parts of the world. This
great increase in the state's
population helped cities like
San Francisco to grow and
prosper at an astonishing rate.

Below left:
Movie stuntmen perform a demonstration for visitors at Universal Studios in Los Angeles.

Below right:
Hollywood has been the film capital of the world since the early 1900s, and more recently the national center of television production. The awesome growth of the motion picture industry since 1920 has contributed to the real-estate and population booms of the Los Angeles metropolitan area.

year-round outdoor filming. Prosperity continued after the United States entered World War I in 1917, when many factories were set up in California to produce such vital items as ships and rubber goods. The discovery of oil at Signal Hill in 1921 accelerated oil exploration throughout the state.

Thousands of people drifted into California during the Great Depression of the 1930s, looking for work and for homes. Some of them were victims of the long drought that created the Dust Bowl, which led to the loss or abandonment of many mid-American farms. In 1935–36 California held the California-Pacific International Exposition in San Diego, followed by the Golden Gate International Exposition on Treasure Island in San Francisco Bay (1939–40).

When the United States entered World War II in 1941, California manufacturers were prepared to produce airplanes, ships, and weapons. Indeed, the state became the aircraft center of the country. And San Francisco became the chief port for troopships going to the Pacific theater of operations.

After the war, California continued to grow. In the 1960s its population increased by some 1,600 persons a day. In 1964 it became the most populous state in the nation and it remains so today. Both San Francisco and Los Angeles have serious air pollution problems. Air pollution control districts have been created and a control has been placed on automobile emissions.

In order to control spending, in 1978 Californians approved Proposition 13 legislation that reduced property taxes by more than half and required a two-thirds majority in popular vote to impose any new local nonproperty taxes. Similar legislation has been adopted in other states.

California today is still a state of extremes. Only 80 miles apart are the lowest and highest points in the lower 48 states—Death Valley and Mount Whitney. Ski areas contrast with blistering deserts, mountains with beaches. California has giant redwoods and giant missiles, Spanish missions and skyscrapers, and the oldest living things on earth—a stand of bristlecone pines said to be 4,600 years old.

Education

The first school in California, the California Academy of Sciences, was established in 1853 in San Francisco following the gold rush. The oldest institution of higher education in the state is the publicly funded University of California, which was chartered in 1868. Originally Berkeley was the only campus; now there are eight, well-organized campuses. In addition, there are a number of private institutions of higher education in the state of California.

The People

More than 95 percent of Californians live in metropolitan areas, such as Los Angeles–Long Beach and San Francisco–Oakland. About 78 percent of all Californians were born in the United States. Of those born in other countries, Mexicans are the most numerous. Roman Catholics make up the largest religious group. Protestant groups prominent in the state are the Baptists, Episcopalians, Methodists, Presbyterians, and Unitarians. Jews form another large religious body.

California's capital city, Sacramento, by night. The state has more than 35 cities with populations greater than 100,000—more than any other state in the nation.

A Mexican woman dances in a traditional festival costume. The Spanish and Mexican cultures have had a strong influence on California history. The area's first white settlers were of Spanish or Mexican origin, and the Hispanic population is still predominant today.

Probably more entertainment celebrities come from California than from any other state—undoubtedly because of the movie industry there. But many non–show-business people from the Golden State have made their mark as well.

Richard Milhous Nixon, the 37th president of the United States, was a native of Yorba Linda and spent much of his life in Whittier and San Clemente. During his terms in office, his achievements were largely in foreign policy, resulting in improved relations with China and the Soviet Union. The scandal surrounding the Watergate break-in, a politically oriented burglary that was planned and supported by the Nixon White House, culminated in the president's resignation on August 9, 1974. He was the first U.S. president to resign his office.

Famous People

Many famous people were born in the state of California. Here are a few:

Bert Acosta 1895-1954, San Diego. Aviator and aeronautical engineer

Annette Adams 1877-1956, Prattville. Attorney and judge

Ansel Adams 1902-84, San Francisco. Photographer

Robert Aitken 1864-1951, Jackson. Astronomer

Gracie Allen 1906-64, San Francisco. Film and television comedienne

Herb Alpert b. 1935, Los Angeles. Grammy Award-winning trumpeter and composer: *A Taste of Honey*

Juan Alvarado 1809-82, Monterey. Governor of Mexican California

Luis Alvarez 1911-88, San Francisco. Nobel Prize-winning physicist

Jack Anderson b. 1922, Long Beach. Pulitzer Prize-winning columnist

Eve Arden 1912-91. Mill Valley. Emmy Award-winning television and film actress: *Our Miss Brooks, Mildred Pierce*

Gertrude Atherton 1857-1948, San Francisco. Author: *The Californians, The Conqueror*

Meredith Baxter-Birney b. 1947, Los Angeles. Television actress: *Family Ties*

Willard Beatty 1891-1961, Berkeley. Educator

David Belasco 1853-1931, San Francisco. Playwright and producer

Candice Bergen b. 1946, Beverly Hills. Television and film actress: *The Group, Oliver's Story, Murphy Brown*

Busby Berkeley 1895-1976, Los Angeles. Choreographer and film director

Chuck Berry b. 1926, San Jose. Rock and roll singer and songwriter

Lloyd Bridges b. 1913, San Leandro. Film and television actor: *High Noon, Sea Hunt*

John Brodie b. 1935, San Francisco. Football quarterback

Dave Brubeck b. 1920, Concord. Pianist and composer

Don Budge b. 1915, Oakland. Tennis champion

Leo Buscaglia b. 1924, Los Angeles. Educator and author: *Living, Loving & Learning, The Fall of Freddie the Leaf*

John M. Cage 1912-92, Los Angeles. Composer

Kirk Cameron b. 1970, Panorama City. Television actor: *Growing Pains*

Gary Carter b. 1954, Culver City. Baseball player

Richard Chamberlain b. 1935, Beverly Hills. Film, stage, and television actor: *The Three Musketeers, Dr. Kildare*

Marge Champion b. 1925, Los Angeles. Dancer and

actress

Cher b. 1946, El Centro. Academy Award-winning film actress and singer: *Moonstruck, Mask*

Julia Child b. 1912, Pasadena. Television chef and cookbook author

Maureen Connolly 1934-69, San Diego. Tennis champion

Jackie Cooper b. 1921, Los Angeles. Film actor: *Skippy, The Champ*

William Cooper 1882-1935, Sacramento. U.S. commissioner of education

Harvey Corbett 1873-1954, San Francisco. Architect

James Corbett 1866-1933, San Francisco. First Marquis of Queensberry heavyweight boxing champion

Kevin Costner b. 1955, Los Angeles. Film actor: *Field of Dreams, Dances with Wolves*

Frederick Cottrell 1877-1948, Oakland. Chemist and inventor

Buster Crabbe 1908-83, Oakland. Olympic gold medal-winning swimmer and film actor

Alan Cranston b. 1914, Palo Alto. Senate leader

Joe Cronin 1906-84, San Francisco. Hall of Fame baseball player and American League president

David Crosby b. 1941, Los Angeles. Rock singer

Ted Danson b. 1947, San Diego. Television and film actor: *Cheers, Three Men and a Baby*

Eric Davis b. 1962, Los Angeles. Baseball player

Glenn Davis b. 1924, Claremont. Football player

Ronald Dellums b. 1935, Oakland. Congressman

Joan Didion b. 1934, Sacramento. Novelist: *Play It as It Lays, A Book of Common Prayer*

Joe DiMaggio b. 1914, Martinez. Hall of Fame baseball player

James Doolittle 1896-1993, Alameda. Soldier and airman in World War II

Thomas Dorgan 1877-1929, San Francisco. Cartoonist and sportswriter

Don Drysdale 1936-93, Van Nuys. Hall of Fame baseball pitcher

Robert Duvall b. 1931, San Diego. Academy Award-winning film actor: *Tender Mercies, The Godfather*

Isadora Duncan 1878-1927, San Francisco. Dancer

Clint Eastwood b. 1930, San Francisco. Film actor: *A Fistful of Dollars, Dirty Harry*

Clair Engle 1911-64, Bakersfield. Senate leader

Joseph Erlanger 1874-1965, San Francisco. Nobel Prize-winning physiologist

Nanette Fabray b. 1920, San Diego. Tony Award-winning stage actress: *Love Life*

Mia Farrow b. 1945, Los Angeles. Film actress: *Rosemary's Baby, Hannah and Her Sisters*

Tom Fears b. 1923, Los Angeles. Hall of Fame

football player

Dianne Feinstein b. 1933, San Francisco. U.S. senator

Sally Field b. 1946, Pasadena. Academy Award-winning film actress: *Norma Rae, Places in the Heart*

Robert Frost 1874-1963, San Francisco. Four-time Pulitzer Prize-winning poet: *New Hampshire, Collected Poems, A Further Range, A Witness Tree*

Frank Gifford b. 1930, Bakersfield. Hall of Fame football player and sports announcer

Sharon Gless b. 1943, Los Angeles. Television actress: *Cagney and Lacey*

Rube Goldberg 1883-1970, San Francisco. Pulitzer Prize-winning cartoonist

Lefty Gomez 1908-89, Rodeo. Hall of Fame baseball pitcher

Pancho Gonzalez b. 1928, Los Angeles. Tennis champion

Gail Goodrich b. 1943, Los Angeles. Basketball player

Farley Granger b. 1925, San Jose. Film actor: *Rope, Strangers on a Train*

Linda Gray b. 1940, Santa Monica. Television actress: *Dallas*

Merv Griffin b. 1925, San Mateo. Entertainer and television producer

Tony Gwynn b. 1960, Los Angeles. Baseball player

Gene Hackman b. 1931, San Bernardino. Film actor: *The French Connection, The Conversation*

Merle Haggard b. 1937, Bakersfield. Country and western singer

Harry Hamlin b. 1951, Pasadena. Television actor: *Studs Lonigan, L.A. Law*

The Hearst San Simeon State Historical Monument was built as a home by William Randolph Hearst, Sr., a wealthy newspaper publisher. At one point in his life, Hearst owned 26 newspapers, 16 magazines, 11 radio stations, 5 news services, and 1 movie company.

Tom Hanks b. 1956, Oakland. Academy Award–winning film actor: *Philadelphia, Forrest Gump*

Edith Head 1907-81, Los Angeles. Fashion designer

William Randolph Hearst 1863-1951, San Francisco. Publisher

Harry Heilmann 1894-1951, San Francisco. Hall of Fame baseball player

Carla Hills b. 1934, Los Angeles. Lawyer and U.S. secretary of housing and urban development

Dustin Hoffman b. 1937, Los Angeles. Two-time Academy Award-winning film actor: *Kramer vs. Kramer, Rain Man*

Sidney Howard 1891-1939, Oakland. Pulitzer Prize-winning playwright: *They Knew What They Wanted, The Silver Cord*

Timothy Hutton b. 1961, Malibu. Academy Award-winning film actor: *Ordinary People*

Shirley Jackson 1919-65, San

Jack Kemp, a former quarterback for the Buffalo Bills, served as the secretary of housing and urban development during the Bush administration.

Francisco. Novelist and short-story writer: *The Haunting of Hill House,* "The Lottery"

Hiram Johnson 1866-1945, Sacramento. Senate leader

Jack Jones b. 1938, Hollywood. Pop singer

Spike Jones 1911-65, Long Beach. Bandleader

Pauline Kael b. 1919, Petaluma. Film critic

Diane Keaton b. 1946, Los Angeles. Academy Award-winning film actress: *Annie Hall, The Godfather*

Jack Kemp b. 1935, Los Angeles. Football quarterback and U.S. secretary of housing and urban development

Anthony Kennedy b. 1936, Sacramento. Supreme Court justice

Joanna Kerns b. 1953, San Francisco. Television actress: *Growing Pains*

Willis E. Lamb b. 1913, Los Angeles. Nobel Prize-winning physicist

Jesse Lasky 1880-1958, San Jose. Film producer

Vicki Lawrence b. 1949, Inglewood. Emmy Award-winning television actress: *The Carol Burnett Show, Mama's Family*

Ursula LeGuin b. 1929, Berkeley. Novelist: *The Lathe of Heaven, The Dispossessed*

Janet Leigh b. 1927, Merced. Film actress: *Psycho,*

Touch of Evil

Mervyn LeRoy 1900-87, San Francisco. Film director and producer

Malcolm Lockheed 1887-1958, Niles. Aircraft manufacturer and inventor

Jack London 1876-1916, San Francisco. Novelist: *The Call of the Wild, The Sea-Wolf*

Anita Loos 1888-1981, Sissons. Novelist: *Gentlemen Prefer Blondes*

George Lucas b. 1944, Modesto. Film director: *American Graffiti, Star Wars*

Ross Macdonald 1915-83, Los Gatos. Novelist: *The Moving Target, The Barbarous Coast*

Clarence Mackay 1874-1938, San Francisco. Businessman and philanthropist

Judah Magnes 1877-1948, San Francisco. Religious leader and educator

Billy Martin 1928-89, Berkeley. Baseball manager

Tony Martin b. 1913, San Francisco. Pop singer

Stephen Mather 1867-1930, San Francisco. Conservationist

Bob Mathias b. 1930, Tulare. Two-time Olympic gold medal winner in the decathlon

Johnny Mathis b. 1935, San Francisco. Pop singer

Joel McCrea 1905-90, Los Angeles. Film actor: *Foreign Correspondent, Palm Beach Story*

Hugh McElhenny b. 1928, Los Angeles. Hall of Fame football player

Rod McKuen b. 1933, Oakland. Poet and composer: *Listen to the Warm, Lonesome Cities*

Edwin M. McMillan 1907-91, Redondo Beach. Nobel Prize-winning physicist

Liza Minnelli b. 1946, Los Angeles. Academy Award-winning film actress: *Cabaret, The Sterile Cuckoo*

Addison Mizner 1872-1933, Benicia. Architect and real

estate entrepreneur

Marilyn Monroe 1926-62, Los Angeles. Film actress: *How to Marry a Millionaire, Some Like It Hot*

Helen Wills Moody b. 1905, Centerville. Tennis champion

Emma Nevada 1859-1940, near Nevada City. Operatic soprano

Richard Nixon 1913-94, Yorba Linda. Thirty-seventh president of the United States

Isamu Noguchi 1904-88, Los Angeles. Sculptor

Ryan O'Neal b. 1941, Los Angeles. Film actor: *Love Story, Paper Moon*

George S. Patton 1885-1945, near Pasadena. U.S. Army General during World War II

Gregory Peck b. 1916, La Jolla. Academy Award-winning film actor: *To Kill a Mockingbird, The Yearling*

Michelle Pfeiffer b. 1957, Santa Ana. Film actress: *Married to the Mob, The*

Fabulous Baker Boys

Bonnie Raitt b. 1949, Burbank. Grammy Award-winning country and western singer: *Nick of Time*

Robert Redford b. 1937, Santa Monica. Film actor: *Butch Cassidy and the Sundance Kid, The Sting*

Sally K. Ride b. 1951, Encino. Astronaut

Robert Ripley 1893-1949, Santa Rosa. Newspaper feature artist, creator of *Ripley's Believe It or Not*

John Ritter b. 1948, Burbank. Emmy Award-winning television actor: *Three's Company*

Cliff Robertson b. 1925, La Jolla. Academy Award-winning film actor: *Charly, PT-109*

Josiah Royce 1855-1916, Grass Valley. Idealist philosopher

Pete Rozelle b. 1926, South Gate. Football commissioner

William Saroyan 1908-81, Fresno. Pulitzer Prize-winning playwright and novelist: *The Time of Your Life, The Human Comedy*

Robert P. Scripps 1895-1938, San Diego. Newspaper publisher

Tom Seaver b. 1944, Fresno. Baseball pitcher

Zoot Sims 1925-85, Inglewood. Saxophonist

O. J. Simpson b. 1947, San

Duke Snider was playing with the Brooklyn Dodgers when the team moved to Los Angeles, the city of his birth.

Francisco. Hall of Fame football player

Duke Snider b. 1926, Los Angeles. Hall of Fame baseball player

Suzanne Somers b. 1946, San Bruno. Television actress: *Three's Company*

Robert Stack b. 1919, Los Angeles. Emmy Award-winning television and film actor: *The Untouchables, The High and the Mighty*

Lincoln Steffens 1866-1936, San Francisco. Journalist and political reformer

John Steinbeck 1902-68, Pulitzer and Nobel Prize-winning author: *The Grapes of Wrath, Of Mice and Men*

Adlai E. Stevenson 1900-65, Los Angeles. Politician and government official

Irving Stone 1903-89 San Francisco. Novelist: *Lust for Life, The Agony and the Ecstasy*

Darryl Strawberry b. 1962, Los Angeles. Baseball player

Lynn Swann b. 1952, Foster City. Hall of Fame football player

Shirley Temple b. 1928, Santa Monica. Child film actress and U.S. ambassador

Gwen Verdon b. 1925, Los Angeles. Two-time Tony Award-winning stage actress, dancer, and singer: *Damn Yankees, Redhead*

Bill Walton b. 1952, La Mesa. Basketball player

Earl Warren 1891-1974, Los Angeles. Chief Justice of the Supreme Court

Ted Williams b. 1939, San Diego. Hall of Fame baseball player

Paul Winfield b. 1941, Los Angeles. Television actor: *Julia, Roots: The Next Generation*

Colleges and Universities

There are many colleges and universities in California. Here are the more prominent, with their locations, dates of founding, and undergraduate enrollments.

Academy of Art College, San Francisco, 1929, 2,009

Art Center College of Design, Pasadena, 1930, 1,221

Azusa Pacific University, Azusa, 1899, 1,974

Biola University, La Mirada, 1908, 2,065

California College of Arts and Crafts, Oakland, 1907, 1,071

California Institute of Technology, Pasadena, 1891, 910

California Lutheran College, Thousand Oaks, 1959, 1,834

California Polytechnic State University, San Luis Obispo, San Luis Obispo, 1901, 15,175

California State Polytechnic University, Pomona, Pomona, 1938, 16,525

California State University, Bakersfield, Bakersfield, 1965, 3,925; *Chico,* Chico, 1887, 13,458; *Dominguez Hills,* Carson, 1960, 7,036; *Fresno,* Fresno, 1911, 15,279; *Fullerton,* Fullerton, 1957, 20,241; *Hayward,* Hayward, 1957, 10,606; *Long Beach,* Long Beach, 1949, 23,584;

Los Angeles, Los Angeles, 1947, 20,804; *Northridge,* Northridge, 1958, 23,093; *Sacramento,* Sacramento, 1947, 19,406; *San Bernardino,* San Bernardino, 1960, 9,192

Chapman University, Orange, 1861, 1,658

College of Notre Dame, Belmont, 1851, 752

DeVry Institute of Technology, City of Industry, 1983, 2,112

Fresno Pacific College, Fresno, 1944, 679

Golden Gate University, San Francisco, 1901, 2,029

Humboldt State University, Arcata, 1913, 6,872

Loyola Marymount University, Los Angeles, 1865, 3,956

Master's College, Newhall, 1927, 819

Mills College, Oakland, 1852, 774

Mount St. Mary's College, Los Angeles, 1925, 1,156

National University, San Diego, 1971, 3,966

Occidental College, Los Angeles, 1887, 1,620

Pacific Union College, Angwin, 1882, 1,509

Pepperdine University, Malibu, 1937, 2,726

Point Loma Nazarene College, San Diego, 1902, 2,035

Pomona College, Claremont, 1887, 1,389

Saint Mary's College of California, Moraga, 1863, 2,306

San Diego State University, San Diego, 1897, 24,162

San Francisco State University, San Francisco, 1899, 19,335

San Jose State University, San Jose, 1857, 23,463

Santa Clara University, Santa Clara, 1851, 4,079

Sonoma State University, Rohnert Park, 1960, 6,089

Stanford University, Stanford, 1885, 6,564

United States International University, San Diego, 1952, 1,570

University of California at Berkeley, Berkeley, 1868, 21,841; Davis, Davis, 1906, 17,508; Irvine, Irvine, 1965, 13,888; Los Angeles, Los Angeles, 1919, 23,649; Riverside, Riverside, 1954, 7,217; San Diego, La Jolla, 1959, 7,217; Santa Barbara, Santa Barbara, 1891, 14,857; Santa Cruz, Santa Cruz, 1965, 9,264

University of LaVerne, La Verne, 1891, 3,886

University of Redlands, Redlands, 1907, 1,465

University of San Diego, San Diego, 1949, 3,914

University of San Francisco, San Francisco, 1855, 3,919

University of Southern California, Los Angeles, 1880, 14,708

University of the Pacific, Stockton, 1851, 3,491

West Coast University, Los Angeles, 1909, 900

Western State University, College of Law of Orange County, Fullerton, 1966, 377

Westmont College, Santa Barbara, 1940, 1,317

Whittier College, Whittier, 1901, 1,159

Where To Get More Information
California Office of Tourism
P.O. Box 9278, T98, Dept. 1003
Van Nuys, CA 91409
Or Call 1-800-862-2543

Hawaii

   The state seal of Hawaii, adopted in 1959, has a shield in the center. To the left stands Kamehameha I, and to the right the Goddess of Liberty holding the Hawaiian flag in her right hand. The sun rises behind the shield and "1959" appears above it. At the bottom is the Phoenix surrounded by taro leaves, banana foliage, and sprays of maidenhair fern. The state motto and "State of Hawaii" are printed in the outer circle of the seal. When color is added, it becomes the state coat of arms.

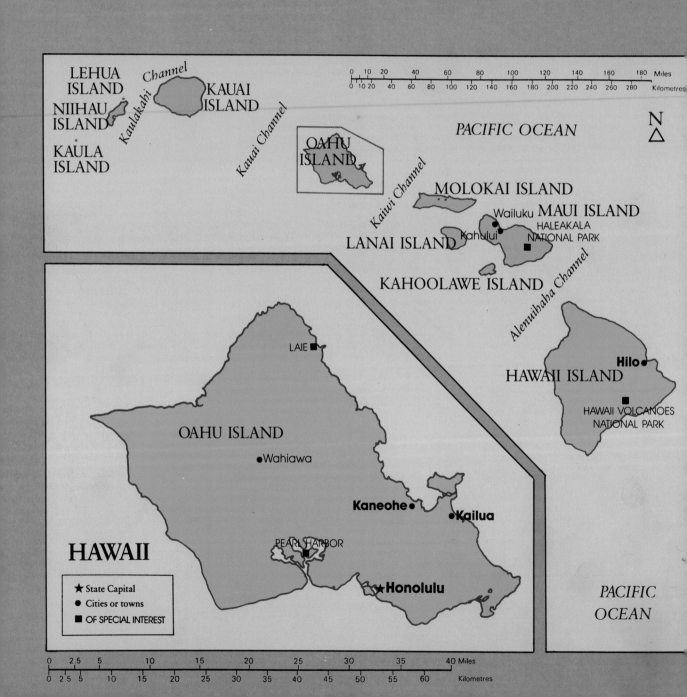

LEHUA ISLAND

Channel

KAUAI ISLAND

NIIHAU ISLAND

Kaulakahi

KAULA ISLAND

Kauai Channel

OAHU ISLAND

PACIFIC OCEAN

N
△

MOLOKAI ISLAND

Kaiwi Channel

Wailuku MAUI ISLAND

Kahului HALEAKALA NATIONAL PARK

LANAI ISLAND

KAHOOLAWE ISLAND

Alenuihaha Channel

Hilo

HAWAII ISLAND

HAWAII VOLCANOES NATIONAL PARK

LAIE

OAHU ISLAND

●Wahiawa

Kaneohe●

●Kailua

PEARL HARBOR

PACIFIC OCEAN

HAWAII

★Honolulu

★ State Capital
● Cities or towns
■ OF SPECIAL INTEREST

0 10 20 40 60 80 100 120 140 160 180 Miles
0 10 20 40 60 80 100 120 140 160 180 200 220 240 260 280 Kilometres

0   2.5   5   10   15   20   25   30   35   40 Miles
0   2.5 5   10   15   20   25   30   35   40   45   50   55   60   Kilometres

HAWAII
At a Glance

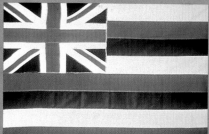

State Flag

State Flower: Hibiscus

Capital: Honolulu

State Bird: Nene (Hawaiian Goose)

Major Crops: Pineapples, avocados, flowers, sugar cane, coffee

Major Industries: Agriculture, food processing, cattle ranching, petroleum, tourism

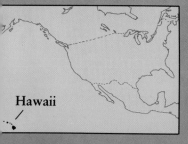

Hawaii

Size: 6,471 square miles (47th largest)
Population: 1,159,614 (40th largest)

State Tree: Kukui (Candlenut)
Nickname: Aloha State

State Flag

The state flag of Hawaii consists of alternating white, red, and blue stripes representing the eight main islands. The upper left corner contains the Union Jack of Great Britain.

State Motto

Ua mau ke ea o ka aina i ka pono
The translation of the Hawaiian motto is "The life of the land is perpetuated in righteousness." These words were spoken by King Kamehameha III in 1843.

The natural beauty of the Hawaii islands is accented by a rainbow arching over Wailua Falls.

State Capital

Honolulu has been the official capital of the islands since 1845.

State Name and Nicknames

The origin of the state name is not known. It may have come from Hawaii Loa, the traditional discoverer of the islands, or from Hawaiki, the traditional Polynesian homeland. "Hawaii" is a combination of two words: *Hawa*, meaning "traditional homeland," and *ii*, meaning "small" or "raging," which may refer to Hawaii's volcanoes.

Since 1959, Hawaii has been officially known as the *Aloha State*. Other nicknames include *Paradise of the Pacific* for its natural beauty, the *Pineapple State* for its pineapple industry, and the *Youngest State* because it was the last state to join the Union.

In addition to the state nicknames, seven of the eight main islands have their own unofficial nicknames.

Hawaii is known as the *Big Island* because it is the largest in the chain. Maui, the *Valley Island,* has many canyons dominating its landscape. Molokai is called the *Friendly Island* for the courtesy shown to visitors by its inhabitants. Since Lanai is owned by the Dole Company, it is often referred to as the *Pineapple Island. The Gathering Place* is the nickname of Oahu, the center of Hawaiian life for nearly 80 percent of the state's residents, and millions of tourists who visit each year. The lush greenery and spectacular beauty of Kauai give rise to its nickname, the *Garden Island.* Niihau, the *Forbidden Island,* is privately owned. It is inaccessible to visitors without the owners' permission.

State Fish

The *humuhumunukunuku-a-pua'a*, or rectangular triggerfish, has been the state fish since 1985.

State Tree

The kukui, also known as candlenut, *Aleurites moluccana*, was named state tree in 1959.

State Bird

The nene, or Hawaiian goose, *Nesochen sandwicensis* or *Bernicata sandwicensis*, was designated state bird in 1957.

State Flower

In 1923, Pua Aloalo, or yellow Hibiscus Bracken-ridgei, was selected official flower. In addition to the state flower, each of the islands has an official flower: Red Lehua, or Ohia (Hawaii); Lokelani, or Pink Cottage Rose (Maui); White Kukui Blossom (Molokai); Hinahina, or Beach Heliotrope (Kahoolawe); Kaunaoa, or Yellow and Orange Air Plant (Lanai); Ilima (Oahu); Mokihana, or Green Berry (Kauai); and, White Pupu Shell (Niihau).

State Languages

Although many others are spoken in the islands, Hawaii's official languages are English and Hawaiian. There are only 12 letters in the Hawaiian alphabet: *a, e, i, o, u, h, k, l, m, n, p,* and *w.* It is one of the world's most musical tongues.

State Marine Mammal

In 1979, the humpback whale was named Hawaii's state marine mammal.

State Song

"Hawaii Ponoi," with words by King Kalakaua and music by Henry Berger, was adopted as state song in 1967. It means "Hawaii's own."

Population

The population of Hawaii in 1992 was 1,159,614, making it the 40th most populous state. There are 101.37 persons per square mile.

Industries

The principal industries of the state are tourism, sugar refining, pineapples and diversified agriculture, aquaculture, fishing, motion pictures, scientific research, and publishing. The chief manufactured products are sugar, canned pineapple, clothing, processed foods, and printing.

Agriculture

The chief crops of Hawaii are sugar, pineapple, macadamia nuts, fruits, coffee, vegetables, melons, and floriculture, especially orchids. Hawaii is also a livestock state. There are estimated to be some 214,000 cattle and calves, 36,000 hogs and pigs, and 1.18 million chickens on its farms. Crushed stone and cement are important mineral products, and commercial fishing earned approximately $70.2 million in 1992.

The sight of a whale frolicking in the ocean is not uncommon for the island inhabitants of Hawaii.

Government

The governor and lieutenant governor are elected for four-year terms. Other top officials, including the attorney general, comptroller, and finance director, are appointed by the governor with the approval of the senate. The state legislature, which meets annually, consists of 25 senators and 51 representatives. The senators are elected from 25 senatorial districts for four-year terms; the representatives are elected from 51 representative districts for two-year terms. The present constitution, which took effect in 1959, was originally approved in 1950 when Hawaii was still a territory. It was modified in 1968 and 1978, and by 1984, seventy-five amendments had been added to the document. In addition to its two U.S. senators, Hawaii has two representatives in the U.S. House of Representatives and four votes in the electoral college.

Sports

Hawaii is a state involved in many sports and activities. On the collegiate level, football's Aloha Bowl is played each year in Honolulu's Aloha Stadium, as is the Hula Bowl. On the professional level, the National Football League Pro Bowl Game, matching the National Football Conference and American Football Conference all-stars, is also played in Aloha Stadium.

Major Cities

Hilo (population 37,808). The heritage of the "Big Island's" capital city is mostly Japanese. Hilo was founded in 1824 as a center of missionary activity. Today it is primarily a residential city and it is the principal port of the island and the shipping and service center of the sugarcane, fruit, and flower industries. Surrounded by sugarcane plantations and orchards, it is the home of the state's thriving orchid industry.

Located only 30 miles from the active volcano Kilowea, it has become an active tourist center.

Things to see in Hilo:
Akaka Falls State Park, Hawaiian Tropical Botanical Garden, Kaumana Caves, Liliuokalani Gardens Park, Lyman Mission House and Museum, Mauna Kea State Park, Mauna Loa Macadamia Nut Plant, Nani Mau Gardens, and Rainbow Falls.

Honolulu (population 365,272). Although it was sighted by James Cook in 1778, the site of Honolulu was not discovered by a European until 1794 when Captain William Brown of England entered what is now Honolulu Harbor. Honolulu is a Hawaiian word meaning sheltered bay. Declared the capital of the Kingdom of Hawaii in 1850 by King Kamehameha, it is known as the Crossroads of the Pacific because it is a stopping point for ships and planes crossing the ocean.

Encompassing the island of

This view of the Honolulu skyline shows that the state is not composed entirely of beaches.

Oahu, Honolulu was a minor village before 1800, and it grew because of its superior harbor and it prospered in the early and mid-19th century as a result of the sandalwood and whaling trades. When Pearl Harbor was attacked on December 7, 1941, Honolulu became the only U.S. city to be bombed in the 20th century.

Tourism is the city's most important industry and approximately 5 million tourists visit Honolulu annually. Honolulu's economy also depends on military activities. It is the center of U.S. military operations in the Pacific, and the air force, army, navy, and Marine Corps all have bases here.

The rapid growth of Honolulu has created housing shortages, high building costs and limited space. In fear of overexpansion, a limit has been placed on hotel construction in certain areas.

This thriving metropolis is a city of contrasts, with its high-rise hotels and condominiums and its beautiful beaches, yet it still retains its ancient exotic charm.

Places to visit in Honolulu: Bishop Museum, Contemporary Museum, Dole Cannery Square, Foster Botanic Garden, Hawaii Maritime Center, Honolulu Academy of Arts, Iolani Palace State Monument, Kamehameha Schools, Kawaiahao Church, King Kamehameha's Statue, Lyon Arboretum, Mission Houses Museum, Neal S. Blaisdell Center, Nuuanu Pali State Wayside, Our Lady of Peace Cathedral, Paradise Park, Punahou School, Queen Emma Summer Palace, State Capitol, Diamond Head State Monument, Honolulu Zoo, Queen Kapiolani Hibiscus Garden, Waikiki Aquarium, Royal Gallery, and the U.S. Army Museum of Hawaii.

Occasionally a volcano on Hawaii erupts with angry abandon as Puu O'o in Hawaii does in this picture.

Places To Visit

The National Park Service maintains 7 areas in the state of Hawaii: Haleakala National Park, Hawaii Volcanoes National Park, Kalaupapa National Historical Park, Kaloko-Honokohau National Historical Park, Puuhonua o Honaunau National Historical Park, Puukohola Heiau National Historic Site, and the USS *Arizona* Memorial. In addition, there are 23 state recreation areas.

Haleiwa (Oahu): Waimea Falls Park. This 1,800-acre park

features an arboretum, botanical garden, diving shows, and hula performances.

Hana (Maui): Waianapanapa State Park and Cave. The water in this cave periodically turns red because of numerous tiny red shrimp. But, according to legend, it is caused by the blood of a murdered Hawaiian princess.

Hanalei (Kauai): Waioli Mission House. This two-story house, built by Reverend William P. Alexander, was one of the first American-style homes on the island.

Honaunau (Hawaii): The Painted Church. The first Catholic church on the island contains elaborate murals depicting scenes from Biblical history.

Kaanapali (Maui): Whaler's Village Museum. A complete skeleton of a sperm whale is the centerpiece of this museum.

Kailua Kona (Hawaii): Atlantis Submarines. Underwater voyages allow visitors to explore the variety of life found in the area.

Kalaheo (Kauai): Olu Pua Botanical Gardens. A plantation house built in 1931 stands in the center of twelve-and-a-half acres of gardens filled with exotic plants and palm trees.

Kaneohe (Oahu): Byodo-In Temple. This replica of a 900-year-old Japanese temple is set beneath the cliffs of the Koolau Mountains.

Kilauea (Kauai): St. Sylvester's Roman Catholic Church. This octagonal church, constructed of lava rock and wood, contains frescoes by Jean Charlot.

Koloa (Kauai): Spouting Horn. A geyser-like effect is formed as wave action forces water through a hole in a lava formation.

Lahaina (Maui): The Wo Hing Temple and Museum. Built in 1912, this restored building contains rare Chinese artifacts.

Laie (Oahu): Polynesian Cultural Center. This 35-acre re-creation of a group of South Seas island villages allows visitors to sample a variety of cultures.

Lanai City (Lanai): Garden of the Gods. This assortment of odd geologic formations, caused by erosion, changes color with the setting sun.

A whale skeleton is prominently exhibited in this whaler's village on Lahaina, Maui.

Lihue (Kauai): Kauai Museum. The history of Kauai, "The Garden Isle," is explored in this two-building complex.

Mahukona (Hawaii): Lapakahi State Historical Park. The remains of houses and canoe sheds can be seen in this 600-year-old Hawaiian settlement, which has been recently excavated.

Maunaloa (Molokai): Molokai Ranch Wildlife Park. This 800-acre preserve is home to 400 species of African and Asian animals.

Napoopoo (Hawaii): Captain Cook Memorial. The memorial, a submerged plaque accessible only by boat, marks the spot where

The Fern Grotto on Kauai island.

Captain James Cook was killed.

Pahala (Hawaii): Punaluu Black Sand Beach Park. The gleaming black sand of the beach was formed when boiling lava poured into the ocean.

Pahoa (Hawaii): Lava Tree State Monument. These tree molds were formed in 1790 when molten lava swept through a grove of ohia trees.

Wailua (Kauai): Fern Grotto. A one-and-a-half-hour boat ride on the Wailua River brings visitors to this beautiful fern-festooned cave, which is a popular site for weddings.

Wailuku (Maui): Maui Historical Society Museum. This museum houses ancient Hawaiian artifacts, and paintings by Edward Bailey.

Waimanalo Beach (Oahu): Sea Life Park. This 62-acre oceanarium offers numerous shows, exhibits, and lectures.

Waimea (Hawaii): Kamuela Museum. This extensive collection of early Hawaiian artifacts includes pieces from the Iolani Palace in Honolulu.

Waimea (Kauai): Waimea Canyon State Park. This 10-mile series of brilliantly colored gorges cut into the Alakai Plateau is inhabited by wild goats.

Aloha Week, held every year in September, features dancing and craft demonstrations.

Events

There are many events and organizations that schedule seasonal activities of various kinds in the state of Hawaii. Here are some of them.

Sports: Kilauea Volcano Wilderness Marathon and Rim Runs (Hawaii Volcanoes National Park, Hawaii), Keiki Fishing Tournament (Kailua-Kona, Hawaii), Bud Light Ironman Triathlon World Championships (Hawaii), Pele's Cup (Mauna Lao, Hawaii), Big Island Ultraman National Championship (Kailua-Kona, Hawaii), Parker Ranch Rodeo and Horse Races (Waimea, Hawaii), Hawaii International Billfish Tournament (Kailua-Kona, Hawaii), Archer's Invitational Tournament and Black Deer Hunt (Waimea, Kauai), Hepthalon Fitness Celebration (Poipu Beach, Kauai), Hanalei Stampede (Hanalei, Kauai), Haleakala Run to the Sun (Kahului, Maui), Maui Classic (Lahaina, Maui), LPGA Women's Kemper Open Golf Tournament (Wailea, Maui), Makawao Statewide Rodeo (Maui), Molokai-to-Oahu Outrigger Canoe Race

The Waikiki Shell is a famous outdoor stage on the island of Oahu.

(Maunaloa, Molokai), Triple Crown of Surfing (Oahu), Honolulu Marathon (Honolulu, Oahu), auto racing at Hawaii Raceway Park (Honolulu, Oahu), Outrigger Hotel Top Gun Hydrofest/Pearl Harbor Aloha Festival (Pearl Harbor, Oahu), International Boogie Bodyboard Championships (Oahu), Hawaii Formula 40 World Cup (Honolulu, Oahu), Rainbow Classic (Honolulu, Oahu), Hawaiian Open Golf Tournament (Honolulu, Oahu), Buffalo's Annual Big Board Surfing Classic (Oahu), polo matches at the Hawaii Polo Club (Mokuleia, Oahu), Wahine Bodyboard Championships (Sandy Beach, Oahu), Pro Surf

Championships (Sandy Beach, Oahu), Waikiki Rough Water Swim (Oahu).

Arts and Crafts: Hilo Orchid Society Show (Hilo, Hawaii), Big Island Bonsai Show (Hilo, Hawaii), Hawaii State Horticultural Show (Hilo, Hawaii), Establishment Day Cultural Festival (Kawaihae, Hawaii), Coco Palms Summer Crafts Festival (Wailua, Kauai), Art Maui (Makawao, Maui), Mission Houses Museum Annual Christmas Fair (Honolulu, Oahu), Downtown Christmas Crafts Fair (Honolulu, Oahu), Honolulu Academy of Arts (Honolulu, Oahu), Okinawan Festival (Honolulu, Oahu), Fancy Fair (Honolulu, Oahu), Pacific Handcrafters Guild Fair (Honolulu, Oahu), Sandcastle Building Contest (Oahu), Orchid Show (Honolulu, Oahu).

Music: Karaoke Festival (Hilo, Hawaii), King Kalakaua Kupuna and Keiki Hula Festival (Hawaii), Kapalua Music Festival (Maui), Prince Lot Hula Festival (Oahu), Ukulele Festival (Honolulu, Oahu), Ka Himeni Ana (Honolulu, Oahu), Kanikapila (Honolulu, Oahu), Gabby Pahinui/Atta Isaacs Slack-Key Guitar Fest (Honolulu, Oahu), Queen Liliuokalani Keiki Hula Competition (Oahu),

Honolulu Symphony Orchestra (Honolulu, Oahu), Hawaii Opera Theatre (Honolulu, Oahu).

Entertainment: Lei Day (all islands), Bon Odori Festivals (all Islands), Aloha Week Festivals (all islands), Kona Coffee Festival (Kailua-Kona, Hawaii), Kona Nightingale Race (Kailua-Kona, Hawaii), Almost Golden Lobster Hunt (Kailua-Kona, Hawaii), International Festival of the Pacific (Hilo, Hawaii), Merrie Monarch Festival (Hilo, Hawaii), Establishment Day (Kawaihae, Hawaii), Captain Cook Festival (Waimea, Kauai), Ke Ola Hou Hawaiian Spring Festival (Hanapepe, Kauai), Koloa Plantation Days (Koloa Town, Kauai), Na Mele O'Maui Festival (Lahaina, Maui), Maui Jaycees Carnival (Maui), Barrio Festival (Wailuku, Maui), Pearl Harbor Aloha Festival (Pearl Harbor, Oahu), Festival of the Pacific (Honolulu, Oahu), Hawaii State Fair (Honolulu, Oahu), Hawaii Mardi Gras (Honolulu, Oahu), East-West Center International Fair (Honolulu, Oahu), The Great Hawaiian Rubber Duckie Race (Honolulu, Oahu), Compadres South Pacific Chili Exposition Cookoff (Honolulu, Oahu), Hawaii State Farm Fair (Oahu), Carole Kai International Bed Race and Parade (Waikiki, Oahu), Hawaii Challenge

National Sport Kite Festival and Annual Oahu Kite Festival (Waikiki, Oahu), Kodak Hula Show (Waikiki, Oahu), Christmas Parade (Honolulu, Oahu), Narcissus Festival (Honolulu, Oahu), Punahou Carnival (Oahu), Cherry Blossom Festival (Honolulu, Oahu), Hula Festival (Honolulu, Oahu), The Japan Festival (Honolulu, Oahu), Makahiki Festival (Haleiwa, Oahu), The Young People's Hula Show (Honolulu, Oahu).

Tours: Waipi'o Valley Shuttle and Tours (Kukuihaele, Hawaii), Fern Grotto (Wailua, Kauai), Molokai Mule Ride (Kalaupapa National Historical Park, Molokai), Pony Express Tours (Haleakala National Park, Maui), Blue Hawaiian Helicopters (Kahului, Maui), Lahaina-Kaanapali & Pacific Railroad (Lahaina, Maui), Dole Cannery Square (Honolulu, Oahu), Chinatown Tours (Honolulu, Oahu), Glider Rides (Mokuleia, Oahu), Pearl Harbor Cruises (Pearl Harbor, Oahu).

Theater: Maui Community Arts and Cultural Center (Kahului, Maui), Hawaii International Film Festival (Oahu), John F. Kennedy Theatre (Honolulu, Oahu), Manoa Valley Theatre (Honolulu, Oahu), Ruger Theatre (Honolulu, Oahu).

The sun sets on Oahu, the most populous of the Hawaiian islands.

The Land and the Climate

Hawaii is unique in many ways. This state, which is farther south and west than any other part of the United States, is made up of 122 islands. Located in the Pacific Ocean more than 2,000 miles from the U.S. mainland, this string of islands extends for some 1,600 miles. Its total land area, however, is only 6,450 square miles—slightly larger than the state of Connecticut. The islands are divided by geographers into three groups: eight main islands in the southeast, islets of rock in the middle, and coral and sand islands in the northwest. All of the islands were formed by volcanoes located on the ocean floor. The eight main islands, from east to west, are Hawaii, Maui, Kahoolawe, Molokai, Lanai, Oahu, Kauai, and Niihau. People live on seven of these main islands; only Kahoolawe has no permanent residents.

Kilauea erupts on the island of Hawaii. Mauna Loa and Kilauea are the only active volcanoes left in the state. The islands of Hawaii were created hundreds of thousands of years ago by massive volcanic activity along a 2,000-mile-long fault under the Pacific Ocean.

"Green sands" are a rarity found on parts of the island of Hawaii. Because all of the islands were formed by great volcanoes that rose from the ocean floor, much of the state's topography is both unique and dramatic. Molten lava and other volcanic elements created strange land and rock formations, and beaches whose sands range in color from black to white to green.

The dormant volcano Haleakala is the highest point on Maui. The island consists of two volcanic mountain complexes joined by low, flat land. Geologists believe that Maui was once attached to its neighbors Molokai and Kahoolawe.

Hawaii is often called the Big Island because it is the largest in the group, covering 4,021 square miles—almost two-thirds of the total land area of the state. This island was formed by five volcanoes—Kohala in the north, Haualalai in the west, Mauna Kea and Mauna Loa near the center, and Kilauea on the southeastern slope of Mauna Loa. Mauna Kea, at 13,796 feet, and Mauna Loa, at 13,680 feet, are the highest points in Hawaii. Mauna Loa and Kilauea are active volcanoes, and the bubbling lava and fire fountains dancing in the crater of Kilauea attract thousands of visitors. Cliffs rim the northeastern and southeastern coasts of the island, and several waterfalls plunge from their summits into the ocean below. Hawaii's main crop is sugar cane; there are also coffee plantations and cattle ranches in the western section.

Maui is sometimes called the Valley Island, because many canyons cut through the two volcanic mountains that form the island. The highest point on Maui is the dormant volcano Haleakala (10,023 feet high). Its crater is 25 miles around and 3,000 feet deep. Maui has large sugar cane and pineapple plantations.

Iao Needle, on Maui, is an odd formation of volcanic rock found in the mountainous western section of the island.

Kahoolawe is the smallest of the eight main islands and the most unusual. Because it is dry and windswept, no one lives there, and United States Army, Air Force, and Navy installations have used it for target practice.

Molokai is often called the Friendly Island because its people welcome visitors so warmly. Its western section contains a broad, dry plateau with many cattle ranches. Its eastern section is riddled with rugged mountains and deep canyons. The island's central plain has fertile soil that supports numerous pineapple plantations.

Lanai is called the Pineapple Island. It is wholly owned by the Dole Company, and the entire island is one big pineapple plantation.

Oahu is known as the Gathering Place; about 80 percent of all Hawaiians live there. It has two mountain ranges separated by a wide valley: the Koolau Range on the east and the Waianae on the west. The valley between them has many sugar cane and pineapple plantations. On the southern coast, west of Honolulu, the state capital, is Pearl Harbor, one of the best natural harbors in the world. It is coral-free and contains about ten square miles of navigable water behind a mile-wide entrance.

Kauai is also called the Garden Island because of its luxuriant tropical greenery and beautiful gardens. It is roughly circular in shape, with 5,170-foot Kawaikini Peak at the center. One of the world's rainiest places is nearby Mount Waialeale, with an annual rainfall averaging 460 inches. Over the centuries, the rain from this area has flowed into rivers that have worn into the volcanic rock to form canyons. One of them is the 2,857-foot-deep Waimea, with its colorful rock walls reminiscent of the Grand Canyon of the Colorado River.

Niihau is also called the Forbidden Island. (It is privately owned and is not open to the public.) Niihau is almost entirely covered by a huge cattle ranch and is one of the few places in Hawaii where the people still usually speak the Hawaiian language.

The total coastline of the eight main islands is 750 miles. But if the tidal shoreline, including bays, islets, and river mouths, is added, the length is 1,052 miles.

The congenial climate of the Hawaiian Islands is renowned. The islands lie in a subtropical latitude, which means almost no seasonal change and generally warm temperatures, which are moderated by currents from the cold Bering Sea and the constant northeast trade winds. Thus the islands can boast a summer average of 78 degrees Fahrenheit and a winter average of 72 degrees F. The trade winds blowing against the mountain slopes yield enough rainfall, well scattered through the year, to keep everything green. Locally, the rainfall may vary markedly from island to island. On the one hand, there is Mount Waialeale, with 460 inches of rain per year; on the other is the semi-desert on Hawaii, with a mere nine inches per year.

Local temperature variations are modified by altitude. Thus on the island of Hawaii, with its towering peaks, there may be balmy weather along the coast, but cold weather on the high mountain slopes. Snow is not uncommon around these peaks in the winter months.

Surfers travel from all over the world to test their skills in Hawaii's challenging waters.

Outrigger canoeing is a popular sport in the clear, blue waters of Waikiki.

The History

What is now Hawaii was devoid of human life until about 2,000 years ago, when Polynesians (Polynesia means "many islands") sailed here in giant outrigger canoes from other Pacific islands. According to local legends, these people were small and shy, but courageous. About A.D. 1200 another group of Polynesians arrived from Tahiti and seized control of the islands. It is said that the islands were named Hawaii for a chief called Hawaii-loa, who led the Polynesians to the islands. But the name also might be a variation of Hawaiki, which was the legendary name of the Polynesian homeland to the west.

It may be that Spanish, Dutch, or Japanese explorers stopped off at the islands beginning about A.D. 1500, but the first official report of a visit was by Captain James Cook of the British Royal Navy, who landed there in 1778. Cook traded with the natives, who were friendly to him, perhaps believing that he was a god. He named the place the Sandwich Islands for the Earl of Sandwich, England, who was the First Lord of the Admiralty. Cook left after two weeks in the islands, but he returned later that year and was killed there in 1779, when his men came into conflict with the Hawaiians.

Other explorers and traders came to the islands soon after Cook's discovery, bringing livestock, manufactured goods, and plants from their home countries. At that time, there may have been as many as 300,000 Hawaiians living on the islands. But during the early 1800s many of them died of European diseases like measles and smallpox, to which they had no immunity.

At the time that Cook arrived, several local chiefs ruled the islands. One of these chiefs, Kamehameha, became the sole ruler of Hawaii Island after a ten-year war that began in 1782. By 1795, with the help of guns that he had obtained from the white men by trade, he united all the main islands except for Kauai and Niihau, which kept their local chief, Kaumualii. It was not until 1810 that these two islands accepted Kamehameha as their leader.

Twelve-foot plumeria leis adorn a statue of King Kamehameha I, who united the main islands of Hawaii under one rule. In a series of battles during the late 1700s and early 1800s, Kamehameha consolidated his power on the main island of Hawaii and went on to take control of Maui, Molokai, and Oahu. Kauai and Niihau accepted his authority in 1810. Previously, each island had been ruled in relative isolation by an independent chief who was a member of the established ruling family.

The Old School Hall on Oahu was built in 1852 by missionaries. As early as 1820, New Englanders arrived to bring Christianity to the Hawaiian people. In addition to the Protestantism that they taught, these Americans brought with them Western medicine, education, and business practices. They soon gained great influence in government, and by the end of the 19th century, English had become the predominant language of the islands.

Between 1811 and 1830, Hawaii sent vast quantities of aromatic sandalwood to China; money from this trade enabled Kamehameha and his successors to buy guns, clothing, ships, and other goods. In 1813 Don Francisco de Paula Marín, a Spanish settler, wrote home about the wonderful pineapple fruit of the islands, but it was not until the 1880s that pineapple cultivation began on a large scale. The first sugar cane plantation was established in 1835 at Koloa on Kauai.

During the 19th century, many whaling ships, most of them American, made port in Hawaii. These ships needed fresh water and supplies, and the Hawaiians earned a great deal of money from the sale of provisions to the whalers.

Liholiho, Kamehameha's son, became King Kamehameha II after his father's death in 1819. He proceeded to abolish the native religion, which included human sacrifice, the worship of images, and a belief in many different gods and goddesses. The following year a missionary from New England, Hiram Bingham, arrived, and he and his fellow missionaries converted most of the natives to Christianity. The first Roman Catholic missionaries came in 1827, but by then Protestantism was the official religion, and the priests were forced to leave in 1831.

Those Hawaiians who had converted to Catholicism were thrown into prison. In July 1839 a French frigate, *L'Artémise,* blockaded Honolulu and the captain, C. P. T. Laplace, declared that he would shell the town if the Catholic prisoners were not freed. The Hawaiians gave in and granted Catholics religious freedom.

The first Hawaiian constitution was adopted in 1840 and provided for a legislature, consisting of a council of chiefs and an elected house of representatives, and a supreme court. Then, in 1842, the United States recognized the Kingdom of Hawaii as an independent nation. France and Great Britain followed suit the next year.

The Kawaiahao Church on Oahu, built in 1842, is constructed of coral blocks. It contains the tomb of King Lunalilo, who ruled the islands from 1873 to 1874 and initiated trade and military negotiations between the United States and Hawaii. The graves of some of the island's earliest missionaries are in its churchyard.

Primarily as a result of diseases introduced from abroad, the native Hawaiian population continued to decline. From 300,000 when Cook arrived in 1778, it dropped to 108,000 in 1836, then to some 73,000 in 1853. One hundred years after Cook's visit, there were only about 50,000 native Hawaiians left. During the mid-19th century, Hawaii began to become the multiethnic society that it is today. There were not enough natives to work the crops, especially the labor-intensive sugar cane, so plantation owners began bringing in workers from other countries. During the 1850s many Chinese arrived. They were followed by Polynesians from the South Pacific, beginning in 1859, and Japanese, beginning in 1868. Then came Portuguese in the 1870s, and Filipinos, Koreans, and Puerto Ricans in the early 1900s.

In 1874 King Kalakaua, called the Merry Monarch, came to the throne. His reign brought a revitalization of the old Hawaiian customs. The Protestant missionaries had forced earlier kings to prohibit such things as traditional Hawaiian music and the hula (which means "dance" in Hawaiian). But Kalakaua encouraged their revival, and it was during his reign that the custom of wearing grass skirts—an importation from Samoa—began. At the same time, sugar cane planting became a large industry, as did the cultivation of pineapples. (A special strain of Jamaican pineapples had been introduced by a horticulturist, Captain John Kidwell, in 1885). In 1887 the United States was given the exclusive right to use Pearl Harbor as a naval station.

Upon the death of Kalakaua in 1891, his sister, Liliuokalani, assumed the throne. She soon sought more power than was granted by the constitution, and in a bloodless revolution of 1893, she was deposed. The revolution was led by nine Americans, two Britons, and two Germans, with the aid of U.S. Marines and sailors. In 1894 the Republic of Hawaii was formed, and a judge, Sanford B. Dole, became the first—and only—president.

The Hawaiian republic was largely under the control of American businessmen, many of whom wanted Hawaii to become a United States territory by annexation. This was accomplished in 1900, and Dole was appointed the first territorial governor.

When King Kalakaua died in 1891, he was succeeded by his sister, Liliuokalani. The last Hawaiian monarch, Queen Liliuokalani ruled for less than two years. During her reign, she attempted to eliminate many of the restrictions that had been placed on the monarchy and tried to proclaim a new constitution. Her bold actions prompted a bloodless revolution in 1893 that forced her from the throne. A provisional government was then created under the leadership of Sanford B. Dole, who was proclaimed President of the Republic of Hawaii in 1894.

Before the United States entered World War I in 1917, construction of the huge U.S. Navy base at Pearl Harbor had begun, and the U.S. Army began establishing camps near Honolulu. During the war, two regiments of the Hawaiian National Guard were called into regular service.

Hawaii continued to blossom after the war ended in 1918. Its economy was on the rise. Then came December 7, 1941, when warplanes of the Japanese Navy made a surprise attack on Pearl Harbor and the airfields on Oahu, resulting in heavy losses of American lives, ships, and aircraft. This officially forced the United States to enter World War II, which had begun in Europe in 1939, when Nazi Germany attacked Poland. Pearl Harbor was later repaired, as were Hickham Field, Schofield Barracks, and other military installations. Hawaii became the headquarters for military operations in the Pacific, while remaining under martial law from 1941 to 1944.

Hawaii had long desired to become a state of the Union. Between 1903 and 1959, no fewer than 59 bills calling for statehood had been presented to the United States Congress. Most of them, however, were

Iolani Palace, on Oahu, was built as a residence for King Kalakaua in 1879–82 and later became the state capitol. It is the only "royal palace" in the United States. Kalakaua, known as the "Merry Monarch," was renowned for his strong will and his ambition to lead a Polynesian empire.

not even voted upon. Not until 1946 did a U.S. President, Harry S Truman, urge Congress to vote for statehood. In 1949 the Hawaiian territorial legislature began to set up a constitutional convention to prepare a document that would go into effect if the territory became a state. Hawaiian voters and their legislature approved the constitution in 1950. But it was not until 1959 that the United States Congress approved legislation to admit Hawaii to the Union: Hawaii became the 50th state on August 21 of that year. The people of the islands at last had full United States citizenship, including the right to vote in presidential elections.

Since that time, Hawaii has boomed. The tourist industry is an ever-growing source of revenue, and food processing remains a major industry. Orchid-growing and flower-packaging have prospered with improved transportation to the mainland. This jewel of the Pacific has become one of the most desirable spots on earth because of its magnificent climate, its natural beauty, and its relaxed way of life. Hawaii's deep blue seas, brilliantly colored flowers, graceful palm trees, ominous volcanoes, and plunging waterfalls comprise some of the most dramatic scenery in the United States. And the Hawaiian reputation for friendliness is summed up in the word *aloha*, which means not only welcome and farewell, but love.

Education

The first U.S. secondary school founded west of the Mississippi River was started in 1840 in Punahou, located on the island of Oahu. It was founded when Protestant missionaries influenced King Kamehameha III to assume responsibility for educating Hawaii's youth. Hawaii is one of the few states in the U.S. in which elementary and secondary schools are completely controlled by a state agency. The University of Hawaii is a state-sponsored institution whose main campus is in Honolulu. It has more than 20,000 students enrolled and

Above:
Honolulu, on Oahu, is Hawaii's capital city. Although the island accounts for less than 10 percent of the land area of the state, nearly 80 percent of the state's population lives here. More than 760,000 people make their homes in the Honolulu metropolitan area.

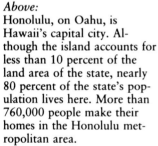

Above right:
Hawaii's population includes more than five major ethnic stocks, including Caucasian, Chinese, Filipino, Hawaiian, and Japanese. More than 30 percent of the population is of mixed racial ancestry.

charges a moderate tuition. There are four private colleges in the state: Chaminade University, operated by the Society of Mary; Brigham Young University, operated by the Mormon church; Hawaii Loa College, established by a group of Protestant churches; and Hawaii Pacific College.

The People

About 75 percent of the people of Hawaii live in metropolitan areas. Approximately 85 percent of Hawaiians were born in the United States. Hawaiians are proud that their state is a mixture of people from diverse ethnic groups including the native Hawaiians (descendants of the original Polynesians), and those whose ancestors came to the islands much later, from China, Japan, the Philippines, Europe and mainland America. Intermarriage has helped to unify these various peoples. Roman Catholics make up the largest religious group. Other large denominations are the Baptists, Buddhists, Episcopalians, Lutherans, Methodists, and members of the United Church of Christ.

The native Hawaiians came to the islands from Polynesia, the collective name for the numerous mid-Pacific islands that take in a huge area from Hawaii in the north to New Zealand in the south and Easter Island far to the east. They were—and are—a handsome, outgoing people who were originally farmers and fishermen. In the few centuries since Captain Cook's discovery of their Stone Age culture, they have moved into the mainstream of Western civilization without losing their deep feeling for family ties, the world of nature, and their native traditions, which have become widespread. We have the Hawaiians to thank for the *lei* (garland of flowers) and the *luau* (an outdoor feast). In the arts of music and dancing, Hawaiians have contributed the ukulele, the Hawaiian steel guitar, and the *hula*, whose movements recall ancient legends and describe the beautiful scenery of the islands. Singer Don Ho has helped to popularize Hawaiian music around the world.

Almost half the people of Hawaii today are of Caucasion ancestry and roughly a third are of Japanese ancestry. The crowded streets of Honolulu, one of the great ports of the Pacific, reflect the rich mixture of races and customs that make Hawaii unique among the states.

Below left:
A group of women string *leis*, garlands of flowers traditionally used as gifts of welcome and honor. Hawaii's abundant flowers allow lei makers to produce brightly colored, exotic necklaces of exquisite beauty.

Below:
Dancers perform the "Lion Dance" for one of Hawaii's many annual festivals.

Famous People

Many famous people were born in the state of Hawaii. Here are a few:

Kamehameha I succeeded in unifying most of the islands in 1796, establishing a dynasty that would last for almost one hundred years.

William D. Alexander 1833-1913, Honolulu, Oahu. Historian and scientist

Samuel Armstrong 1839-93, Maui. Educator

Henry Baldwin 1842-1911, Lahaina, Oahu. Sugar grower and capitalist

Hiram Bingham 1831-1908, Honolulu, Oahu. Missionary to Micronesia

Henry Carter 1837-91, Honolulu, Oahu. Merchant and diplomat

William Castle 1878-1963. Honolulu, Oahu. Diplomat and author

Ron Darling b. 1960, Honolulu, Oahu. Baseball pitcher

Walter Dillingham 1875-1963, Honolulu, Oahu. Business executive

Sanford Dole 1844-1926, Honolulu, Oahu. President of the Republic of Hawaii and governor of the Territory of Hawaii

Sid Fernandez b. 1962, Honolulu, Oahu. Baseball pitcher

Erin Gray b. 1952, Honolulu, Oahu. Television actress: *Buck Rogers in the 25th*

Century, Silver Spoons

John Gulick 1832-1923, Waimea, Kauai. Missionary, naturalist, and writer on evolution

Luther Gulick 1865-1918, Honolulu, Oahu. Educator

William Hillebrand 1853-1925, Honolulu, Oahu. Chemist

Don Ho b. 1930, Kakaako, Oahu. Singer and entertainer

Charlie Hough b. 1948, Honolulu, Oahu. Baseball pitcher

Daniel K. Inouye b. 1924, Honolulu, Oahu. Congressman

Duke Kahanamoku 1890-1968, near Waikaiki, Oahu. Three-time Olympic gold medal-winning swimmer

Jonah Kalanianaole 1871-1922, Kauai. Delegate to Congress from Hawaii

Kamehameha I 1758-1819, Kohala district, Hawaii. Founder and first monarch of unified Hawaii

Jesse Kuhaulua b. 1944, Hawaii. Champion sumo wrestler

George Lathrop 1851-98, near Honolulu, Oahu. Author and editor: *Rose and Rooftree, Spanish Vistas*

Queen Liliuokalani 1838-1917, Honolulu, Oahu. Last monarch of the Hawaiian Islands

Mike Lum b. 1945, Honolulu, Oahu. Baseball player

Ellison Onizuka 1946-86, Kealakekua, Kona, Hawaii. Astronaut

Poncie Ponce b. 1933, Maui. Television actor: *Hawaiian Eye*

Red Rocha b. 1923, Hilo, Hawaii. Basketball player

Don Stroud b. 1937, Honolulu, Oahu. Television actor: *Mickey Spillane's Mike Hammer*

Lorrin Thurston 1858-1931, Honolulu, Oahu. Lawyer and editor

Milt Wilcox b. 1950, Honolulu, Oahu. Baseball pitcher

Colleges and Universities

There are several colleges and universities in Hawaii. Here are the most prominent, with their locations, dates of founding, and enrollments.

Brigham Young University— Hawaii Campus, Laie, Oahu, 1955, 2,064

Chaminade University of Honolulu, Honolulu, Oahu, 1955, 2,610

Hawaii Pacific College, Honolulu, Oahu, 1965, 6,976

University of Hawaii at Hilo, Hilo, 1970, 2,675; *at Manoa,* Honolulu, Oahu, 1907, 19,810; *West Oahu,* Pearl City, 1976, 700

Where To Get More Information

Hawaii Visitors Bureau
2270 Kalakaua Avenue
Honolulu, HI 96815
Or Call 1-808-923-1811

Further Reading

General

Grabowski, John F. and Patricia A. Grabowski. *State Reports: The Pacific.* New York: Chelsea House, 1992.

California

Bean, Walton. *California: An Interpretive History,* 3rd ed. New York: McGraw Hill, 1978.

Beck, Warren A., and Williams, D. A. *California: A History of the Golden State.* New York: Doubleday, 1972.

Carpenter, Allan. *California,* rev. ed. Chicago: Childrens Press, 1978.

Caughey, John W. *California: A Remarkable State's Life History,* 3rd ed. Englewood Cliffs, NJ: Prentice-Hall, 1970.

Curry, Jane L. *Down from the Lonely Mountain: California Indian Tales.* New York: Harcourt, 1965.

Fradin, Dennis B. *From Sea to Shining Sea: California.* Chicago: Childrens Press, 1992.

Johnson, William W. *The Forty-Niners.* New York: Time Inc., 1974.

Lavender, David S. *California: Land of New Beginnings.* New York: Harper, 1972.

Lavender, David S. *California: A Bicentennial History.* New York: Norton, 1976.

Loftis, Anne. *California— Where the Twain Did Meet.* New York: Macmillan, 1973.

Rolle, Andrew F. *California: A History,* 2nd ed. New York: Crowell, 1969.

Rolle, Andrew F., and Gaines, J. S. *The Golden State: A History of California,* 2nd ed. AHM, 1979.

Sanderlin, George W. *The Settlement of California.* New York: Coward, 1972.

Starr, Kevin. *California! A History.* Peregrine Smith, 1980.

Stein, R. Conrad. *America the Beautiful: California.* Chicago: Childrens Press, 1988.

Suggs, Robert C. *The Archaeology of San Francisco.* New York: Crowell, 1965.

Terrell, John U. *The Discovery of California.* New York: Harcourt, 1970.

Hawaii

Bianchi, Lois. *Hawaii in Pictures.* Sterling, 1979.

Carpenter, Allan. *Hawaii,* rev. ed. Chicago: Childrens Press, 1979.

Fradin, Dennis B. *Hawaii in Words and Pictures.* Chicago: Childrens Press, 1980.

Gray, Francine du P. *Hawaii: The Sugar-Coated Fortress.* New York: Random House, 1972.

Joesting, Edward. *Hawaii: An Uncommon History.* New York: Norton, 1972.

McNair, Sylvia. *America the Beautiful: Hawaii.* Chicago: Childrens Press, 1989.

Marsh, Carole. *Hawaii & Other State Greats.* Decatur, Georgia: Gallopade Publishing Group, 1990.

Simpich, Frederick, Jr. *Anatomy of Hawaii.* New York: Coward-McCann, 1971.

Wallace, Robert. *Hawaii.* New York: Time Inc., 1973.

Photo Credits

Courtesy of James Blank: pp. 11, 15; Courtesy of California Office of Tourism: pp. 3, 7, 17, 18, 25, 30, 31, 32, 33, 34, 35, 36, 37, 38, 40, 42-43, 48, 50, 51; Courtesy of California Secretary of State: p. 5; Courtesy of Gilroy Garlic Festival/Bill Strange: p. 27; Courtesy of Hawaii Visitors Bureau: pp. 4, 61, 63, 69, 71, 72, 74, 76, 77, 78, 80, 81, 83, 84, 85, 88, 90, 91; Courtesy of Hawaii Visitors Bureau/Anthony Anjo: p. 73; Courtesy of Hawaii Visitors Bureau/Peter French: pp. 64-65; Courtesy of Hawaii Visitors Bureau/Dan R. Salden: p. 67; Courtesy of Hawaii Visitors Bureau/Greg Vaughn: p. 70; Courtesy of Hearst San Simean/John Blades: p. 55; Courtesy of Los Angeles Convention & Visitors Bureau: pp. 8-9, 14; Courtesy of Mann's Chinese Theatre: p. 19; Museum of the American Indian: p. 39; National Portrait Gallery, Smithsonian Institution: pp. 45, 87; Courtesy of the New York Mets: p. 58; New York Public Library: p. 92; New York Public Library/Stokes Collection: pp. 46-47; Courtesy of Office of President Nixon: p. 52; Courtesy of the *Queen Mary*: p. 20; Courtesy of San Francisco Convention & Visitors Bureau: p. 16; Courtesy of Santa Barbara Convention & Visitors Bureau: p. 23; Courtesy of Tournament of Roses: pp. 13, 28; Courtesy of Universal City Studios/Peter C. Borsari: p. 24; Courtesy of U.S. Department of Housing and Urban Development: p. 56; Courtesy of Winchester Mystery House: p. 22; Courtesy of Winners' Circle Ranch: p. 21.

Cover photos courtesy of California Office of Travel and Tourism and Hawaii Office of Travel and Tourism.